KISSING PRINCETON CHARMING

C.M. SEABROOK

FRANKIE LOVE

for aj!

xofrankie

"Things just got royally complicated."

We have reputations for a reason.

His?
Spencer Beckett:
Princeton Charming. Ivy League
    Playboy. Rich AF.

Hers?
Charlotte Hayes:
Campus sweetheart. Virgin. Working
    her booty off to get through this
    last semester.

When a bet pushes these two together it's fire and
    ice ... and Charlotte is melting. Fast.

But Charlotte has a chip on her shoulder. She
doesn't believe that fairy tales exist in the real world.

One kiss tells her this is a bad idea.

Two kisses tells her he's too good to
be true.

Three kisses and she's royally screwed.

Spencer Beckett might be everyone else's Prince Charming but can he sweep this princess off her feet?

SPENCER

IT's the same old shit. Another political party camouflaged as a good cause. A fundraiser for some housewife's charity that no one here gives a damn about. An excuse for these rich fuckers to dress in their Brioni suits and Versace dresses, and make themselves feel like they're more superior than the college kids they're paying minimum wage to serve us champagne and caviar.

I should be writing the essay I have due next week on civil procedure, not rubbing elbows with the Princeton elite, but family protocol demands that at least one Beckett attend these events. Since my parents are currently in Washington with their noses stuck up some rich senator's ass, trying to get my dad re-elected to office, the responsibility fell on me.

Everything falls on me now.

I take a sip of champagne and try not to let the familiar ache in my chest take root. It should be Ethan here. He was the one my parents groomed to take over the family political empire. He played the part well. Enjoyed every second in the spotlight. And I was more than happy to let my big brother play king of the castle because, in fairness, *princes* have a hell of a lot fewer responsibilities.

But two years ago today, the dumbass decided to snort several lines of coke before getting behind the wheel of the Porsche my parents bought him for his twenty-second birthday.

That old familiar knife digs into my chest, opening old wounds, and letting guilt trickle out. I slam back the rest of the champagne, and look around the room, needing something stronger to get me through the rest of the night.

"Jesus, Spencer, haven't seen you look so fucked since your parents brought Winslow to Nantucket last year." Prescott Addington is my oldest friend and can read me better than anyone else. And he's right. Being here is the last place I want to be. I'm good with a party. I just prefer the ones where I can freely flirt, hook-up and make an exit as soon as my cock desires.

A place where I'm not worried about running into Winslow Harrington, the woman my parents have been dead set on marrying me off with since I was barely out of diapers. Usually she's on my arm at these types of events, playing the perfect girl-friend, even though it's all a sham. But I'm so sick and tired of playing the damn game.

"Where is Winnie, anyway?" Prescott asks, glancing around. "Usually she's tethered to your hip at these things."

"Didn't ask her to come," I mutter.

Prescott whistles low. "She's going to be pissed. So are your parents."

I grunt, hating the eyes of my mother's cronies at this gala that take in every move I make. I have no doubt one of them has already informed my parents that I came here alone, but honestly, tonight I don't care.

The fact that I have to be here at all, on the anniversary of Ethan's death, is bullshit. But then the world I live in, with its plastic smiles and calcu-lated conversations has no room for grief.

Prescott hands me a drink and I take the glass of amber liquid, sniffing it before draining the aged scotch, glad for the rush of numbing heat that races down my throat and into my veins.

"Here, have another," he says, grabbing a random glass off a passing waitress' tray and replacing it with my empty one.

I smirk and down the contents. "You trying to get me drunk?"

"No, I just want to have fun tonight and you're a serious buzzkill."

"Duly noted." My head is already spinning, but the ache in my chest is still there, which means I haven't had nearly enough to drink. I have no doubt Prescott has something stronger tucked away in his suit pocket, but I swore off the white stuff after being called in to identify my brother's body.

Another thing I have to be grateful to my parents for since they'd been out of the country at the time.

I dig my palm into my temple and try to push away the images that will be forever burned in my memory. The only thing I'm grateful for is that my younger sister Ava didn't have to see him the way I did.

"Hey," Prescott says to a server that's walking past. When she doesn't respond, he snaps his fingers and says louder, "Hey beautiful. We need some drinks over here."

From behind, there's nothing special about the girl. Tiny, at least compared to me, with a slender waist, and slim hips. I wouldn't give her a second glance, but I'm not prepared for the eyes that turn and meet my gaze.

Too damn big for her head, that's my first thought. Hazel with flecks of gold, green, hell, I think I see every color swirling there. Lined with thick, dark lashes, they dominate her pixie-shaped face. High cheekbones, turned-up nose, shoulder length hair that's chopped and styled in a way that makes her look like she just rolled out of bed.

One look and I know I wouldn't mind her rolling out of *my bed*.

She's not traditionally beautiful, but there's something about her, a confidence despite her unpolished appearance, that intrigues me. But it's the recognition in those multi-colored eyes, the way her spine straightens and her lips pull down that has my curiosity piqued.

"You look familiar. Do I know you?" I ask.

I can feel the eye-roll she holds back, sense the comment she bites her tongue on before she gives a shake of her head. But her gaze is still fixed on me, and I can feel the tug, the gravitational pull. And even though it's clear she's trying to hide it, I see her pupils dilate, the way she pulls her bottom lip between her teeth, nervously. I even catch her letting her gaze drop down to my chest before she looks away, cheeks turning a cute shade of pink.

Her gaze diverted, I let my own skim down her body. White blouse, black dress pants, typical of what the other servers are wearing, they do nothing to accentuate the soft curves I have no doubt are hiding under the material.

"Funny. I swear I've seen you around." I give her an easy, practiced smile, one that got me the nickname Princeton Charming, and add with a slight tilt of my head, "Maybe in my dreams?"

It's silent, but I hear her inward groan. But despite taking a step back, she tilts her chin to me, and asks stoically, "Do you need something?"

Maybe it's the alcohol, or the need to numb the pain that still presses against my chest, but I push, despite the clear *fuck off* sign she has posted on her forehead. "I need whatever you're offering, sweetheart."

She scoffs, but there is the tiniest hint of a smile on her pink, pouty lips. "You're ridiculous, Spencer Beckett."

"So, you know my name." I step toward her. "Doesn't seem fair, I don't know yours."

She twists her lips, those expressive hazel eyes swirling with intensity. "I think we know enough about each other."

"I know nothing about you..." I take another step toward her, feel the undeniable electricity that sizzles between us, not caring that the room is filled with watching eyes that will no doubt report back to my parents. I grin down at the girl. "Except that you're gorgeous."

Prescott snorts behind me.

She glances around me, taking in my friend, then back to me, a new fire in her eyes. But this time it's anger and not desire that fuels it.

"Are you seriously hitting on me when I'm working?" Her eyes scan my body again, but there's a hint of disgust in her voice, like my appearance offends her. "You are——" Her lips clamp down on whatever she was about to say.

Pretty sure it was going to be an insult, which only intensifies my intrigue.

Even I can hear the slight slur of my words when I say, "I want to know more about you."

Her eyes narrow, and she says sarcastically,

"Princeton Charming wants to know more about me."

Prescott coughs, and says under his breath, "About what you'd look like in his bed."

She ignores him, gaze still fixed on me. "Okay, fine. You know that I'm a waitress, which means I'm broke, which means I'm not your type. I didn't grow up on Martha's Vineyard and my idea of a work ethic is pulling up my bootstraps."

"So..." Deadpanned, I lift my brows. "You're saying you've got a chip on your shoulder?"

Prescott chuckles, and I'm about ready to turn and tell him to fuck off, because I'm seriously enjoying this little banter. For the first time in a long while, I feel something more than numb guilt, I feel...fire. Because that's what this girl is -- passion and stubbornness.

And it doesn't hurt that she's cute as hell.

"Well?" I push, knowing how this will go down. Her in my bed before the night is over.

Lowering her chin, she bites the side of her lip, and takes a steadying breath before continuing, "I'm saying I've got work to do." She lifts her tray to make a point. "And you..." She gives a shake of her head. "Need to work on those pick-up lines of yours." Without another glance, she sashays away, and my cock twitches with want.

"Damn, Spencer, you're losing your charm," Prescott says behind me. "The great Princeton Charming is shut down."

I just shove my hands in my trouser pockets and try to keep my gaze from following the girl around the room. The game is only starting. Her walking away only makes me want her more.

"She's not typically my type, but I'll do the grunt work..." Prescott grins at me, then lets his gaze drift back to the girl.

I know what he means, that he's willing to share her. It wouldn't be the first time. But something possessive coils in my stomach at his suggestion, and I don't want her anywhere near him.

"If you're into her," he adds, a grin tugging at his lips and a knowing look in his eyes. "I can—"

"I'm not," I lie.

"Bullshit. You were practically undressing her with your eyes. And like I said, I'm in, if you want me to—"

"No." It's a command rather than a response, and Prescott's brows shoot up. But I can see right away that he takes it as a challenge. "Fuck," I mutter as he begins to saunter over to the far corner of the room where she's restacking her tray with glasses of champagne.

I'm about to go after him when the girl's eyes flick over to mine, then back to Prescott. I see her ask him something and he frowns, resting a hand on her arm as he answers.

What the fuck is he doing?

Prescott leans in and kisses her on the cheek before walking back to me. My hands are fists and I'm ready to take this outside where no prying eyes can document the moment I push my oldest friend against the wall.

"What the hell was that?" I ask, my words tense and my voice low.

"It was me smoothing things over, getting you a second chance to make a first impression."

"Yeah? And how did you manage that?" I ask, my eyes narrowing.

"I told her you were having a rough night. That it's the anniversary of your brother's death. I was pulling the sympathy card."

"You're a callous bastard, you know that? And I don't need your help to get her into bed."

"Is that so?" He grins, one brow cocked. "Shall we bet on it?"

"You're such a fucking ass." Mostly, because he knows I have a hard time turning down a bet.

"True." Prescott laughs. "So that's a yes?"

"What kind of bet?"

"If you can't manage to get her to go home with you tonight, then you owe me a night in Atlantic City. Hookers. Blow. As many hands of blackjack as I want."

"And if I win—"

He cuts me off. "Then you, my friend, can continue your reign as Princeton Charming." He raises his hands. "Plus the night in Atlantic City, on me."

"What's in it for you?"

He chuckles. "Watching you make an ass of yourself with a woman who clearly doesn't want you is priceless."

2

CHARLIE

As I MOVE around the room with a tray of champagne, I know I'm being watched. One conversation with Spencer Beckett and I understand the appeal. It's his ability to take a step closer, look into your eyes, and use lines that no other man on campus could say without sounding dumb.

Princeton Charming. I get why he got the nickname. Even drunk, which he clearly is, the man oozes sex appeal. Maybe it's because he's six-foot-one, built, and stands with the kind of confidence I dream about, like he owns the place.

And hell, maybe he does. This gala is taking place in the Presidential Wing at the University. Everyone knows the Becketts are Princeton Royalty.

And me? I'm a scholarship girl who shoves extra bagels in my backpack when I eat in the dining hall.

Which is why when Spencer weaves his way toward me as I'm refilling my tray for the forty-sixth time, that famous Princeton Charming smile tugging at his lips, I doubt his sincerity.

Tickets to this event were half my monthly paycheck. He doesn't want to talk to me because he's actually interested. He wants to take me to bed. Another notch on his bedpost. And from what I've heard about the man, there isn't much space left.

"So Prescott gave you my sob story?" he asks, leaning against the bar as I carefully place flutes of Prosecco on the tray.

"I'm sorry for your loss," I say, glancing up. "If the story is real."

"You think Prescott would make that up?"

"Isn't that the job of a wing-man?" I don't meet his gaze this time. It's unnerving, those piercing blue eyes. Despite the warmth of them, the invitation and promises of pleasure, there's something else there, something I understand -- pain. But the last thing I need to feel right now is sympathy for one of Princeton's infamous bad boys.

I've made it through to my senior year by

keeping my head down, legs closed, and working every spare minute I'm not studying or sleeping. No matter how many times I've fantasized about one night with Spencer Beckett, I know reality would never live up to my dreams.

"It would be pretty cold. Even for us." He clears his throat as if preparing for something. "Truth is, it's not okay to use my brother's death to get you in bed."

I pause. "So that really was the goal of his little heart-to-heart with me?"

Spencer runs a hand over the back of his neck. "I don't know Prescott's intentions, I just know mine."

"Which are?"

He gives me another one of his dimpled grins. "To take you home and see how snug the glass slipper fits."

I groan. "Is that an innuendo?"

"If you want it to be, Cinderella."

"I don't." I pick up my tray and start to walk away, but he steps in front of me.

"Tell me your name?"

"If I tell you, will you walk away?" My words don't at all mirror my desire. I don't want him to leave, I want him to pull me close. But there is no way I could admit that out loud. It would be a sure-fire way to get hurt.

His eyes twinkle, and I can tell he's enjoying this. "No."

My boss Janice walks by, snapping her fingers. "Charlotte," she hisses. "I pay you to work the room, not fraternize with the guests."

Spencer stands up straighter, turning his grin to Janice, who immediately falls under his spell. "You're Janice Walker, right?"

Obviously frazzled, she lets him take her hand and stutters out a yes.

"I wanted to compliment you. The event is flaw-less." The smile he gives her is different than the one he turned on me. More plastic, like he's playing a role. "My parents will be pleased."

"Wonderful to hear, Mr. Beckett. I—"

"You wouldn't mind giving me and..." He grins at me when he says my name. "Charlotte, a few minutes alone."

"Oh, of course not. Anything else you need, Mr. Beckett, just let me know." Her smile is tight, but she quickly leaves us.

Damn. I know I'm in trouble when he even has

my boss scurrying away to do his bidding. I turn back to my tray, wishing at the same time that he would both go away and come closer. It's been so long since I've had undivided attention from a man. Mostly because I don't have time in my life for guys. For parties. *For fun.*

Maybe it's pathetic, but it feels good to be under his gaze. And even if all he wants is to get in my pants, it gives me a thrill to have the campus hottie's interest for a moment.

"So, Charlie," he says, using a nickname that only my closest friends and parents are allowed to call me. "When do you get off?"

I turn back to him and muster up all my self-preservation. His proximity has my skin prickling with heat. But I lead with my mind, rarely my heart, and I don't intend on changing that for Spencer Beckett of all people.

"Why are you doing this?" I ask him, genuinely curious and honestly confused. He could take home any woman here.

"Doing what?" His words are slurred. Yeah, he's drunk. Is that why he's all over me? It's not like he's ever noticed me before. Not that I've really given him a chance, I prefer the shadows...and this man lives in the sun.

I sigh. "Being so insistent."

"Because I like you." His grin is infectious.

He's playing you, Charlie.

"You don't know me."

"But I want to? You're..." He leans in, and I can smell his cologne, rich and woody, and reminding me of why the man is dangerous. He's just another trust fund brat who's been handed everything to him on a silver platter. "*Gorgeous.*"

"You said that already." I set a hand on my hip, not interested in his objectification of me, even though I am doing the exact same thing. He is so much sexier up close. I've only ever seen him at a distance. Now though, he is right here, close enough to kiss.

Do not think about kissing Spencer Beckett, my brain warns, even though my body is already humming with the possibilities.

And when he reaches out and traces my jaw with the pad of his thumb, I can't help the shiver of need that races through me -- and he sees it.

Shit.

He smiles with a kind of arrogance only money can buy, but the promise of pleasure in his eyes makes me fall a little farther under his spell.

Damn you, Spencer Beckett.

"You want me, Charlie," he practically purrs, his voice smooth and velvety, making my core clench with need.

"My name's Charlotte."

"Charlie seems more appropriate. It suits you. Strong. Stubborn." He holds my chin between his fingers and leans closer. "Yeah, you're definitely a *Charlie*." The nickname rolls off his lips. Lips that are way too close to mine now. "Put that tray down, Charlie, and come with me."

"I-I'm working." I hate that I stutter, that even I can hear the give in my words. Hate that I'm even considering it.

"What do they pay you here? I'll double it. Shit, I'll triple it. Just leave with me now."

Did he really just say that? Proposition me like he can pay me for sex.

When I reach for the glass, I know I'm going to regret it, but the normal, rational part of my brain that has gotten me this far in life, seems to have shut down around him.

I tell myself that it's his proposition that has me flinging the full glass for champagne in his face -- but that's a lie. It's because I'm infuriated with myself. Everything about him should have me stepping away, but my body is begging me to step closer. Practically demanding I lean to his offer.

I don't trust myself.

So instead I throw the liquid gold in his face.

"Oh my God," Janice is back, shocked and horrified.

Honestly, I'm a little horrified too. I'm not the type to act reckless and let my emotions get the best of me.

I'm easy going. I'm practical. The girl with a library card, who rides a bicycle around campus because cars are expensive, and who basically lives in my roommate Daphne's wardrobe because she likes to share and I hate to shop.

This. Is. Not. Me.

Throwing drinks in the face of *The* Spencer Beckett when I'm on the clock at a job that is essential to my survival at an Ivy League school, is not the way my father raised me.

"Charlotte Hayes," Janice seethes. "Come with me. Now." She grabs me by the arm and I barely have time to set my unsteady tray of champagne flutes down on the table before she's dragging me to the kitchen.

I look over my shoulder, my gaze meeting Spencer's. To my shock, he doesn't look angry.

He looks turned on.

And that pisses me off even more.

APPARENTLY THE EASY going girl who rolls with the punches has left the building for the night. My face is streaked in tears and my tote bag rests heavy on my shoulders as I leave through the back door of the gala.

Janice fired me. Deserving? Maybe. Devastating? Absolutely.

But what was I supposed to do? Let that...that arrogant, privileged jerk suggest that he could pay for a night with me. Not in a thousand years. No matter how desperate I am. Which after tonight's little fiasco is pretty desperate.

It's late November, I've only been back to school for a few days since returning from Thanksgiving break. I wanted to go home even though the trip was going to be short. I missed Mom so badly and wanted to make her and Dad a Thanksgiving meal, knowing she wasn't well enough to do it herself.

I'm glad I flew home to Michigan. Mom was sicker than she let on over the phone, and I needed to see it for myself so I could know how to support her. But now, as the icy winter air sweeps over me, I feel numb and doubt my choice. The plane ticket home was the last of my savings, and now that I'm out of a job I'm not sure how I'm going to manage to get back home for Christmas.

I push down the knit hat on my head and dig in my tote for my gloves. My bicycle is across the street, and I shove my hands in the mittens as I step off the curb.

"Charlie!" a voice slices through the dark, icy night, and I'm pulled back to the sidewalk just as an SUV with an Uber sticker in the windshield barrels past me.

"Oh," I cry out, my gloves swept into the wind as I'm pulled back, and I sink against the body of the man who saved me. Startled, I cling to him for a second. "Tha-thank you!"

I turn, his arms wrapping around me, and I look up, needing to see who my knight in shining armor is.

The man staring down at me is no knight.

It's Princeton Charming.

Of course it is.

"It's not midnight, Charlie. You don't need to run away from me so fast."

"You have the worst lines," I say, trying to still

my heart. The rush of the near collision has me gasping, and I'm still in his arms.

"You like it though," he says with a chuckle. He holds onto me without any intention of letting go. I don't mind. In this exact moment, I want to be held.

Just *not* by Spencer Beckett.

"What I like is being treated like a human being, not a piece of meat you think you can buy." I step back, my resolve strengthening as I remember his earlier comment.

"What?" He looks completely confused.

"You offered to pay me...for sex," I remind him.

"Shit. No." He winces and rubs the back of his neck. "That's not what I meant. Charlie, I—"

"Look, you've already done enough tonight." Stupid tears gather in my eyes because I needed that damn paycheck.

I'm about to turn, but he grabs my elbow. His arrogance is gone when I meet his concerned gaze, and my head spins again with his touch. He smells like leather and scotch and spice. It's not a smell I know well, but it's one I like. A lot. Even though I know, I shouldn't.

He's right, I do have a chip on my shoulder. A big one. Because I know people like him. They take, make demands, think every good thing is their privilege, never caring about who they hurt to climb to the top of whatever social ladder they're climbing.

Just like the men at the banks who refused to give my dad a loan to help pay for my mom's medical expenses.

Just like the insurance company that decided to cancel their plan when they found out she was sick.

Just like all the people on this damn campus who have no idea what it's like to hold two part-time jobs while trying to keep up their academic performance so they don't lose their scholarship.

Despite my attempt to blink them back, big, hot tears stream down my cheeks.

"Hey," Spencer says.

Suddenly my face is being held by the most sought-after man on campus, and he uses his thumbs to wipe away my tears. God, those blue eyes, they stare down at me with compassion and lust, and the promise of a night filled with more pleasure than I've ever experienced.

"Jobs come and go, right?" he says easily. "It's not the end of the world. I bet you hated it anyway."

The words cut through the magic of the

moment, and I step back. "Actually, in the *real* world that isn't how jobs work. I needed that job."

"Let me fix things—"

"By what? Propositioning me again?" I laugh, but there's no humor in it. I just need to get away from him. A bike isn't fast enough. But there's a cab coming down the street, and I wave for it to stop, but when I step off the curb as the car approaches, my heel sinks into a drain grate, and when I lift my foot it comes away shoeless. "Damn it."

"Here, let me help…" He leans down the same time I do to retrieve the shoe and our foreheads collide.

"I don't..." I try to yank the shoe out, but it won't budge. "...need...your..." The shoe flies free and I fly backward with it, once again straight into oncoming traffic, and I cry out, "Help."

"Got you." I'm pulled back into his arms, icy water spraying us from the cab that squeals its tires to a stop a couple feet away.

"Jesus, lady," the cab driver yells through the half-open window. "You trying to get yourself killed?"

On shaky legs, I manage to stand. I reach for the door handle of the taxi, practically throwing myself in the car.

"Charlie," he calls out as I slam the door.

Humiliated, frustrated, and an emotional wreck, I don't turn to meet his gaze, not until the cab starts to take off. And when I do, I see Spencer Beckett's perfect frame disappearing behind me, and I groan when I see what he's holding in his right hand.

My damn shoe.

3

SPENCER

DESPITE HOW HARD I TRY, I can't get the girl out
of my head. Maybe it's because I've had her shoe
sitting on my nightstand for the past week, begging
me to find its owner, like a freaking Cinderella story.

But this is no fairy tale. And even though I've
cashed in on my nickname, I'm sure as hell no
Prince Charming. I'm the antithesis of a hero. The
guy who fucks everything up. The deadbeat who'll
never be able to fill his older brother's shoes.

At least according to my dad.

The man likes to remind me whenever he's had
too many bourbons that it should have been me
who drove that car over the cliff and not Ethan.

Fucked up? Yeah. But hearing shit like that
screws with a person's mind. Which is why when

my phone vibrates and I see my mom's number pop up on the screen, I groan inwardly.

But ignoring the woman isn't an option. She'll just keep calling, or worse, hop in her private jet and fly to see me.

"Hey, Mom." I lean against my dresser and pick up the shoe -- *Charlie's shoe.* I can't help but smile thinking that I still have a piece of her. Even if that piece can be replicated at any big box store for less than ten dollars.

My mother's voice is raised an octave and I can hear the outrage seething through her words. "Janice just called me—"

"Janice?"

"The event organizer for last weekend's Gala. She was apologizing profusely, said one of her waitresses attacked you—"

"Charlie didn't attack me."

There's a short pause. "You know the girl?"

No. But I want to. More than I care to admit. "Everything is fine."

"Everything is not fine if one of the staff humiliated you."

"She didn't—"

"I've made sure she's fired, and she won't be getting a job anywhere—"

"Mom." Frustration seeps into my words. "It was me who was out of line."

Her words come out slow, filled with suspicion when she asks, "Out of line how?"

"Charlie..." I catch my reflection in the mirror and wince at the man who stares back at me. A man who falls into all the categories the girl tagged me in. Privileged. Arrogant. Selfish. Asshole. "She thought I propositioned her."

My mom sucks in an outraged breath. "My God, Spencer. How could you?"

"I didn't. It was a misunderstanding."

"You can't afford those kinds of misunder-standings. If the girl knows who you are, and she brings this forward, she could ruin your reputation."

"You mean Dad's reputation. That's what you're really worried about."

"Spencer Thomason Beckett, how dare you speak to me like that?"

"Sorry." I rub my forehead. "I'll deal with it. The girl won't be a problem."

There's a short pause before my mother sighs, and her voice returns to its normal sweet cadence which she's perfected over the years being a politi-cian's wife. "Don't you think it's time you settled down? I was talking with the Harringtons yesterday and they told me that Winslow—"

"Mom."

"You care about her, I know you do."

Of course I do. We've known each other since we were still in diapers, she's like family. But I have no intention of making the woman my wife, no matter how happy it would make my mom.

"At some point, you're going to have to settle down."

Not likely.

"If I ever do, Mom. It'll be my choice."

"You were always such a stubborn child. Why can't you be more like..."

I hear her unspoken word - *Ethan.*

There are moments when I know she forgets he's gone. And I hear it now. The small gasp on the other line as his loss hits her. Grief infuses the silence between us.

"Mom?"

She sniffs, and says softly, "Yes?"

"I love you."

More silence, and when she speaks again, her tone is cold, callous. "Just remember who you are, Spencer. You're a Beckett. Act like one."

She ends the call, and I shove my phone back in

my pocket, wishing that my name didn't feel like a noose around my neck or a damn curse.

I know she's right though. I am a Beckett. Even if my family is dysfunctional, they're still my family. And after everything we've gone through in losing Ethan, I refuse to give my parents another reason to mourn.

Besides being reminded of my familial duty, talking to my mom gave me an idea. I call Janice, the event coordinator, and after several minutes of smooth talking, I'm able to convince her to open Charlie's file for me. Phone number, address, and even a last name, completely confidential and illegal, but I guess there are some benefits to being a Beckett.

One thing I'm not able to do is get her her job back.

"I'm sorry, Mr. Beckett, but your mother insisted—"

"Yeah, I get it." I may have the name, but it's my parents who have the power.

Even over me.

They still have power over my finances, and while I have some of my own money that my grandfather left me, it's barely a drop in the ocean of the Beckett fortune.

"Thank you for your help, Janice," I say. "And I'd appreciate if you'd keep this call between us."

"Of course." I can hear the nerves in her voice before she hangs up. My mother must have laid into her good.

I've been on the receiving end of the woman's lectures enough times that I know how intimidating she can be.

Both my parents thrive on control. Especially over their children. Ethan and Ava were always better at accepting it. Me? There's always been an itch inside me wanting to rebel.

I shouldn't complain. What my mother and father lacked in parental love, they made up for in things.

Gifts. Toys. Anything I want, I always got.

Even this place.

I live in a townhouse in Palmer Square. After living on campus for my freshman year, my needs required more than the typical college experience. I needed a proper bedroom to bring home my conquests.

A bedroom that to my aching cock's dismay hasn't seen any action lately. Even before I couldn't get Charlie out of my head. The whole one-night stand, meaningless sex thing has just gotten old. Not that I'm looking for anything serious.

Shit, I don't even know what I'm looking for. I just know I'm tired of feeling numb. And the only thing that's made me feel alive in a long time is the girl with the eyes too big for her head, and a tongue sharper than an obsidian blade.

Charlie lives on campus, so that's exactly where I head after tucking her shoe in my messenger bag.

After parking my Mercedes-AMG, I turn toward the senior dorms, more than ready to find the girl I've been thinking about for days.

It's the end of fall and the leaves have already changed color. I inhale a deep breath of the crisp air as I walk through the old buildings. God, I love this place. The old stonework, the mature trees, it's like you can feel the history surrounding you, like it's a life force of its own.

To be honest, it's the first place I ever felt at home.

Growing up in boarding schools, traveling summers around Europe, I never felt like I had roots. Sure, the Becketts owned homes. Many of them. Most scattered along the east coast. Washington. The Hamptons. Hilton Head Island. But they're just houses.

The first year here, I knew this was where I wanted to be. Didn't even matter that I was dubbed the *Little Prince* by my brother's frat friends. I took the jabs, proved myself with the jocks, the geeks, the Delta Phis, and each of the sororities, eventually getting re-nicknamed Princeton Charming.

"Hi, Spencer." A pretty blonde waves at me as she walks by, giggling to her friends when I smile back.

I'm a bit of a legend on campus. Sounds cocky, sure, but it's the truth. And I'd be lying if I said I minded the attention. It's a flattering ego boost and some days, like today when I've talked to my mother on the phone, it feels good to be doing something right. Even if that something is walking around campus with a cocky grin.

I find Charlie's door and knock, but it's not big hazel eyes that greet me when it opens, it's a pair of blue ones that go wide when the girl sees me.

"Spencer Beckett," she says, brushing her platinum blonde hair down nervously. "I...uh...hi."

I give her a forced smile and glance over her shoulder, hoping I have the right room.

"I just came to return this." I pull out the shoe. "Is Char—"

"My shoe?" She takes it from me, frowning. "How did you get it?"

"I kinda borrowed them," a familiar voice says behind me.

I turn to meet the eyes I came here for, the ones that I've been fantasizing about for the past few days. And they were worth the wait. Today, they look more amber than hazel, the sunlight that streams through a window hits her face, and I see the splattering of freckles across the bridge of her nose and cheeks.

"How did you find me?" Her pouty lips tug down.

"I have my ways."

Her frown deepens. "So you're a stalker now?"

"Charlotte." Her friend sounds almost panicked, like she can't believe she'd talk to me that way.

And I chuckle, because most people don't.

"I just came here to return your shoe."

"*My* shoe," her friend reminds me, dangling it on one finger and frowning between me and Charlie, but focusing on me more than I'd like.

"Can you give us a minute?" I ask the blonde, pulling out one of my dimpled smiles, then winking. "I'd appreciate it."

With a sigh, she steps back into the room and shuts the door.

"Well, that takes the whole fun out of the shoe fitting," I joke, turning back to Charlie, and meeting the suspicion in her gaze.

"Another innuendo?" she asks, then adds quickly before I can answer, "Thank you for bringing it back. And thank you for..." She grimaces. "For saving me the other night. It doesn't make up for what you said or for getting me fired, but——"

"I didn't mean to offend you. I'd had too much to drink and I didn't mean to imply I was paying you for sex."

A couple girls walk by when I say the words and start to giggle and whisper as they walk away.

"Great," Charlie rolls her eyes. "Any other damage you'd like to do while you're here?"

I'm messing things up, again.

"I talked with Janice, explained to her that it was my fault what happened."

"You did?" Her arms drop to her sides, and she chews on her bottom lip. "So I have my job back?"

I wince. "Not exactly, my mother found out about it, and——"

Charlie groans. "Great. So I'm probably black-listed from every job on campus now."

"Let me help you."

"I don't want your help."

"But you need it. And it would make me feel better."

"Well, if it'll make you feel better," she says, sarcasm dripping from her words. "Then I wouldn't want to stand in the way of the great Princeton Charming."

"You've got a mouth on you."

"You're observant. Most humans do. And last I checked I am one." Her words are quick, but I'm starting to think they're a defense mechanism. I know I have enough of them.

I take a step toward her, see her fidget and the small shaky breath she takes in. "Do I make you nervous?"

"Cocky *and* delusional," she says, taking another step back when I move forward.

"It's okay if I do." I place a palm on the wall beside her head when she's backed against it.

"You don't." She juts her chin up at me, but the small tremble of her bottom lip gives her away.

"Okay." I lean down so that I'm practically eye to eye with her. It'd be so damn easy to steal a kiss, and I know she wants it, I can feel the pull between us, but I have no doubt I'd end up with a hot, red palm print on my cheek. "So what *do* I make you, Charlie?"

She shrugs. "Infuriated. Annoyed. Frustrated." Each word is shaky, and despite the way she's trying to hide it, I see the need in her eyes. She wants me, she's just too stubborn to admit it.

"I haven't been able to stop thinking about you," I say.

"Not used to women turning you down?"

"No. And not used to getting champagne thrown in my face."

Her cheeks turn red. "I doubt that's the first time—"

"It was." I chuckle. "Most people tend to like me."

"Sorry, I'm not dazzled by your sparkling good looks and money."

"Sparkling good looks?" I raise a brow at her.

She moans. "Yes, Spencer, you're hot. But that doesn't mean every girl on campus wants to...to..." More color returns to her cheeks and she looks away.

"Wants to what?" I'm probably enjoying this way too much. "Fuck me?"

"Nice." She starts to move away, but I take her hand, and when my skin meets hers, hell if the whole world doesn't stop spinning.

It's just me and her and a primal need that I've never felt before. A desire that's so intense it scares the shit out of me. And in a heartbeat, I have her back against the wall, this time my body pressed against hers, my fingers in her hair, thigh budged between hers, my breathing ragged as I try to use every last ounce of my self-control from crushing my mouth against hers, and probably destroying any chance I have with this girl.

"I want to kiss you, Charlie."

She whimpers. A sound that makes my already aching cock harder than granite.

"Say yes, Charlie. Let me taste your lips." I'm not past the point of begging with her. I don't kiss. It's one of my rules. But I want, no need to possess her mouth. I lean closer. "Just say yes."

Her bottom lip trembles and she says, "Ye—"

"Charlotte?" a gruff voice says behind me, and I don't need to turn to hear the jealousy in that one word.

Flustered, she places her palms on my chest and pushes me away.

"You okay, Char?" The guy, who I recognize as

Tatum Madden, Princeton's top wide receiver for three years straight, is glaring at me like he's ready to use his hands for more than just catching footballs.

"Yeah...yes." She runs her hands over her torn jeans. "Fine. This is...uh..."

"Spencer Beckett," I say, holding out a hand to him, and wondering if I didn't just make an ass of myself by almost kissing the dude's girlfriend. I have certain rules, no kissing, no stealing another man's girl. But hell, with Charlie, I'd break both of them.

"Yeah, I know who you are." Nostrils flare and muscles tense as he continues to stare daggers at me.

"I should...uh..." Charlie opens her dorm door, not looking at either of us now. "I'll get your laundry, Tatum."

Why the hell does she have his laundry?

Tatum's gaze never falters, he keeps glaring at me. "How do you know Charlotte?"

"We met at a party."

"She doesn't go to parties unless she's with me." There's the jealousy again. She might not be his girlfriend, but it's clear he wants her.

I shrug just as Charlie returns with a basket of neatly folded laundry.

"Thanks Charlotte," Tatum says taking it from her. "I'd be screwed without my special t-shirt for tonight's game."

She smiles up at him. "I know. I used the fabric softener you like too."

I watch the exchange, see the warmth in Charlie's eyes, the lust in Tatum's.

"You'll be at the game?" he asks.

"Of course, I even bought face paint. I'm going all out."

"You're the best." Then he reaches in his back pocket and pulls out an envelope. "Oh, this is for you."

Heat rises to Charlie's cheeks and I'm dying to know what's in that letter. God, since when did I let a jock get under my skin? I'm above all that shit, aren't I?

Tatum squeezes Charlie's shoulder before walking away. I run a hand over my jaw, wondering when I got so damn jealous. But I saw the way Tatum looked at her and it sends some primal signal to my brain. *Make her yours.*

4

CHARLIE

Spencer's gaze is dark, the blue of his eyes piercing when I turn back toward him. There was some weird vibe going on between him and Tatum when I'd come back out with the laundry. Even now, it's hard to read what he's thinking.

You shouldn't care what he's thinking, my brain admonishes. *This is Spencer Beckett. The man is everything I despise.*

But...the *almost* kiss. The heat still lingers between us.

Unconsciously my fingers lift to my lips. I'd wanted it. Still do. But the guy is a player. Worse, he's an arrogant, trust fund brat who thinks he can charm his way into my pants.

Daphne pushes the door open, lips pursed when

she looks between Spencer and me. She seems annoyed with me, but I have no idea what I did wrong. Usually we're on good terms. But then her moods fluctuate so quickly that sometimes I wonder if she should be taking meds for it. The girl can break down in tears one second and the next, be ready to take on the world, or at least the varsity rugby team, which was last month's conquest.

"I'm going to get some food before the game. See you guys later," she says tightly with a small wave.

As she starts to walk away, I look my roommate over. In her thigh high boots and bodycon dress, she looks ready for a nightclub, not a freezing football game. Knowing her, she'll end up skipping the game altogether in lieu of some party. Though in truth, everyone on campus will end up at some party after the game. I promised Tatum I'd be his sidekick tonight, even though I should be studying for the English quiz I have Monday morning.

"Have fun," I say, stepping into my now empty room. Then leaning into the hall, and ignoring the fact that Spencer followed me in, I call after her, "And text me if you need anything, Daph!" I feel like I owe her for something I can't exactly pinpoint. Maybe she's pissed that I borrowed, then lost, her shoe.

Still, that isn't my biggest worry at the moment.

Not when the most notorious man on campus is standing in my bedroom.

This got real, really quickly.

I try to piece together whatever is happening between Spencer Beckett and me. That near-kiss was full of chemistry. I know he felt it. But maybe it's a normal thing for him.

I turn to face Spencer as I close the door, immediately regretting it. But it would just be weird now if I opened it again.

"So you and Tatum, are you a thing?" Spencer asks as he walks around my room, taking it in, his voice laced with something that sounds almost like jealousy.

I smile at the question.

"No. We've never dated," I clarify, watching him as he picks up one of my textbooks, then sets it back down. "But we have been friends since freshman year." I try to suppress my nerves when Spencer's gaze turns to me, but I can hear the small shake in my voice when I say quickly, "We're both scholarship kids, lived on the same floor, and I impressed him with my ability to recite all the lyrics to the *Fresh Prince of Bel-Air* theme song."

"That *is* impressive," Spencer says with that arrogant grin of his. "But so is this record collection." His eyes have fallen on my bookshelves filled with the seven-inch records I've been scouring music shops and thrift stores for since I was twelve-years-old.

"My mom was a piano teacher, she tried to teach me, but failed miserably," I explain. "So she taught me the next best thing. How to listen to music. How to appreciate it. It's one of the greatest gifts anyone has ever given me."

Spencer crouches and flips through the albums. "Shit, some of these are collector pieces."

"You like vinyl?"

"I do," he quips, standing and walking toward me. His eyes are bright, like he sees something he likes, something he wants. It takes me a moment to realize that thing is me.

His hand cups my cheek. "You are an enigma, Charlie Hayes."

I draw in a tight breath. "And you are very smooth."

Wait, how does he know my last name? Or for

that matter where I live. This whole thing is unnerving.

"You like smooth?" His mouth is so close. His lips practically on mine.

God, I want him. But warning bells blare in my head. I should tell him to leave. Instead, I stutter over words, "I've never had smooth." It's the truth. I've had boys kiss me who didn't know what they were doing, sloppy and unremarkable. I've had guys kiss me who were desperate and trying way too hard.

But Spencer Beckett is neither a high school boy nor a clingy college guy. He is something else entirely. He knows what to do as he lifts my chin ever so slightly. As he licks his lips, tempting me to lick my own. His eyes search mine and for a moment I feel found -- or at least seen.

"You said yes before," he rasps, blue eyes searching mine.

I whimper, "I..."

"I'm going to kiss you now, Charlie." His head lowers, and his lips brush against mine before I have a chance to change my mind.

One kiss and I know I'm in trouble.

One taste and I know my resolve is gone.

His tongue presses against mine, my toes curling

and my core tightening. My fingers working on their own accord as I drag them through his thick head of hair. His hand is on the small of my back, his palms strong and steady, keeping me in place.

I forget that I'm a girl who never kisses on the first date. I forget that this isn't even a date. I forget that he's all wrong for me. That he propositioned me. That I walked away.

Because right now there is no refusal, no snarky comments, no playing hard to get. Right now I am jelly in this man's hands.

His phone buzzes. Loudly. Insistent and annoying as hell and we pull apart -- short of breath. Me, panting, noticing the tight strain across his dark denim jeans and I press my knuckles to my mouth, catching my breath as he checks his phone.

"Fucking Prescott." He slides the phone off, pushing it into his pocket, and then reaches for me again, but I'm back in reality.

I just kissed Princeton Charming.

"That was some kiss," he says, looking past me. His eyes are on my bed.

I swallow. Hard. A kiss is one thing. Sex? That's a whole different story and one I'm not ready for. Especially not with Spencer Beckett.

"I have to get ready for the football game."

He lifts his brows. "Really? Because we could stay here and—"

I cut him off. "It's Tatum's final game, senior year. I wouldn't miss it for the world."

He gives me that smile again, tucking a strand of hair behind my ears. "You're only saying that because you've never seen my cock."

I drop my jaw, genuinely shocked. Guessing that line must typically work for Princeton Charming.

He must register my response because his mouth is now on my ear. "Sorry, Charlie," he says. Hot air, soft lips -- my body melts under him. "I don't mean to shock you," he whispers. "I just want to give you the world. Trust me, sweetheart, it'll be worth missing the game for."

"Spencer." I press a hand to his chest, needing to create distance between us. I whimper, realizing just how solid his chest is. It's a rock. A monument of muscle. "I'm not ready...I need..."

He nods, stepping back. "A date?"

"What?" I'm so flustered.

"To the game." He drags his knuckles across my cheek, then sweeps a strand of hair behind my ear. "Do you need a date to the game?"

I exhale, dropping my head. "Um..." *Say, no*

Charlotte, my head demands. "Sure." *Shit. What am I doing?* "That would be...good."

He grins down at me, triumph shining in those blue eyes. Eyes that I have a feeling will be my undoing.

My body has never stirred quite like this. Like I just might forget myself if he keeps touching me. Which he's still doing.

"I....need to get ready."

"You look pretty ready to me."

I hear the innuendo in his words, but when I look up at him, I see he's only teasing. His lips twitch with amusement as he looks me over.

Desire. Heat. A look that's almost primal. And my body aches with the need to give into him.

What harm would it do? What would happen if I gave myself over to him for a few hours? What would it hurt to have a little bit of fun?

I'm strong enough to survive Princeton Charming. But I'm starting to think I'm not strong enough to resist him. Maybe I don't want to.

I lick my swollen lips, press a palm to my hot cheeks, and chew on my bottom lip as I move to my dresser to find my Princeton hoodie.

"If you're gonna be my date," I say, finally calmed down. "Then you need face paint too."

He laughs and shakes his head. "Only for you, Charlie. Only for you."

⸻

AN HOUR LATER, Spencer and I are all decked out in black and orange and walking into Princeton Stadium. It's packed with students and faculty. We're playing Harvard today and one side of the stadium is filled with fans in crimson and gray, and our side is filled with tiger stripes. Just like the ones I painted on our faces.

Usually the season ends in November, but this game is the first weekend of December. The chill in the air seems to bring the festive nature of the event to life. The place is swarming with people, and Spencer reaches for my hand.

"I don't want to lose you," he says against the shell of my ear.

I lift my eyes to meet his, and if we were alone I'd silently beg him for another kiss, but we aren't, everyone on campus is here, and all of these people have an opinion on the man I'm with.

"We have seats in section five," I tell him. He nods, leading the way.

As we weave through the crowd, we're stopped

a dozen times. Everyone looks from him to me, and I notice all the stares, but Spencer either chooses to ignore it or is just living in a different reality. A reality where he can do no wrong, where there are no repercussions for his choices. A world where privilege is king, especially for Princeton Charming.

Kick off happens as we find our seats and for the next three hours, we are caught in a hailstorm of chanting and cheering. Tatum is killing it on the field and I practically lose my voice shouting his number, twenty-three, as he runs in two touchdowns.

Prescott finds us at halftime, delivering popcorn and soda, and handing Spencer a flask.

"In all these years I've never seen Spencer have so much school spirit," Prescott teases.

"Maybe Charlie is a good influence on me," Spencer tosses back.

Prescott smirks. "Call it what you want, Charming. Blackjack is calling my name, motherfucker!" He waves us off, and I ask Spencer what that was all about.

"Prescott is a douche, that's all you need to know."

"I thought he was valedictorian of your graduating class?" I ask.

"You seem to know a lot about him." Is that more jealousy in his voice?

I shake my head. "Not really, just that for all his games he's still impressively smart."

Spencer scoffs. "I take offense, Charlie."

I laugh. "Aww is your ego bruised? You're not happy with being the hottest guy on campus, you need to be the smartest too?"

Spencer laughs as the second half begins. "Right now I'm just happy to be here with you."

5

SPENCER

THE GAME WAS LIT, but the party after is going to be seriously off the hook if the amount of texts I've received over the last hour is any indication. Everyone is going out tonight. We may attend an Ivy League University, but our parties are just as down and dirty as any school's. Tonight is no exception. While the football players and their fan clubs head toward the Tiger Inn, I assume we're going straight to the Ivy.

Once we're out of the stadium I ask Charlie if she wants to grab some food before we go. I'm an eighth generation of the club, my family practically owns the place, and tonight I want to own Charlie. I'm already imagining myself in a big leather chair, pulling her into my lap, returning to the kiss we left off on hours ago.

She furrows her brows. "Um, I won't be going to the Ivy tonight, Spencer. Or ever, most likely."

"Why's that?" I frown. I wouldn't even consider going anywhere else.

"Because it's the most elite eating club on campus. I didn't rush for a reason. It's not my thing. Besides, I promised Tatum I'd meet him at the Tiger Inn."

Trying not to get offended I shrug. "You trying to ditch me, Hayes?"

She rolls her eyes. "No, I'm saying if you want to be my date, come to a real party, at a real club. The Ivy sounds stuck up and boring."

I smile, wrapping my arm around her shoulders. "See, I didn't realize the unassuming Charlie Hayes was such a partier. Now I know."

She laughs. "Maybe I'm not an Animal House level of partier, but I can hold my own pretty well."

I hate sharing her with anyone, especially Tatum Madden, but I see the stubborn tilt of her chin and know that my choice is either her or Ivy. It's an easy choice. I place an arm possessively over her shoulder, not caring who sees and lead her to my car.

The party is in full swing when we pull up to the century-old Tudor-style mansion that's one of the four main eating clubhouses on campus. I get a text from Prescott wondering where the hell I am and write back with a wince that I'm staying at the Tiger Inn with Charlie.

Douchebag: You already pussy whipped?

Me: Fuck off.

Douchebag: No way, asshole. I'm heading there now. Oh, and fyi, Winslow is with me.

Shit. I turn off my phone and shove it in my pocket.

"Everything, okay?" she asks over the hammering of music as we enter.

I give a tight nod, placing my hand on her lower back, feeling overly protective. I'm used to eyes on me, but it's not just me they're staring at now. And I get it, Charlie is gorgeous, but by being here with me, she's also just earned a reputation she doesn't deserve.

I see the smirks from the guys, the way their eyes scan over her like she's prey. See the glares from the girls, the way they peg her as competition. The damage is done, but thankfully Charlie doesn't seem to notice. Or if she does, she doesn't seem to care.

Someone places a cup of foaming beer in Charlie's hand, and when she starts to take a sip, I take it from her.

"Hey." She pouts up at me.

"You should know better than to drink something someone just hands to you."

"You're my dad now?"

I frown down at her. "I'm serious. There are guys who would put shit in—"

"There's my girl." Tatum comes up behind Charlie, and sweeps her up, spinning her around until she's smacking his chest and telling him to put her down.

It's clear the guy has already been drinking, his eyes are glassy, and he's got an even dopier look on his face when he grins down at *my girl*.

"That was a great game." Charlie smiles up at him with the familiarity of old friends. Seeing them together, I'd think there was something going on between the two of them, but she doesn't look at him the way she was looking at me earlier.

"Where's your drink?" Tatum asks, starting to pull her away "We have to get you--"

"Uh, wait." She glances over at me, but I catch

a familiar face in the crowd and a blonde ponytail that quickly disappears out the back door.

Shit. What is she doing here?

"Spencer, do you want anything?" Charlie asks, but my focus is no longer on her. It's on the trouble that just disappeared around the corner.

"No." I give her a tight smile before turning and following the ponytail outside.

When I catch up to the girl, I grab her arm and twist her around. Green eyes widen when they land on me.

"Spe-Spencer. What are you doing here?"

I grunt, glaring down at my sister. "I'm here with a friend, because I'm legally allowed to be." I take the plastic cup from her hand and toss it into a nearby bush. "Are you kidding me with this stuff?"

"God, Spence, you're worse than Mom and Dad."

"Because Mom and Dad don't give two shits what you do. You're only—"

"Nineteen. I'm not a kid, I don't need you watching out for me."

Except I can already hear the slur in her words.

"Come on," I take her elbow. "I'll drive you back to your dorm."

"No." She yanks her arm back and a few heads

turn in our direction, including Charlie who has come out on the deck with Tatum. She frowns at me before turning and walking back inside.

"I'm staying here," Ava slurs, pouting up at me.

I glance back to where Charlie disappeared, feeling a tug, and not knowing what to do, but when I turn back to my sister, she's already slipped away.

"Damn it," I mutter, moving back inside. I know Ava is right. I was doing a lot worse at her age. And I'm not her father, even though I know our own will have my balls if I ever let anything happen to her.

I search the large house, but my sister is gone, or at least dodging me. And Charlie is surrounded by Tatum and his jock friends when I find her in the great room.

"Sorry, I had to deal with that," I say, pulling her away from the looming giant who is way too handsy with her.

"Girlfriend troubles?" Her gaze is hard, and she takes a sip from a new plastic glass she's acquired.

I sigh. "Ava's my sister."

"Oh." She tugs her lips between her teeth and looks slightly embarrassed. "I didn't know you have a sister. She's cute."

"She's trouble. And considering she's never had

any real supervision, she thinks she can do whatever she wants."

"Perks of being Princeton royalty, I guess."

"You think I'm the same?"

"Aren't you?" Her brows raise. "What have you ever wanted that you haven't gotten?"

"You." I lean closer, and grin. "But I'm working on it."

I see her tremble, feel the heat rise between us.

"Princeton Charming." Tatum's words are slurred as he wraps a large arm around Charlie's waist, and I see her flinch. "You look like you could use a drink," he hollers over his shoulder. "Someone bring the prince a bourbon." He looks back at me. "That's what you rich folks drink, right? Or do you plan on slumming it with us tonight with some warm beer and cheap whiskey?"

I don't have a chance to respond. Slim arms wrap around my waist, and the scent of expensive perfume fills my nostrils as a blonde leans into me, staggering so that I have to hold her up from falling.

"Spencer," she whines. "I knew you'd find me."

"Winslow?" I push her chin up to see her face, but her eyes are half masked, pupils pinpricks, mascara smudged beneath. "Jesus."

"Another sister?" Charlie asks, but I hear the sarcasm in the question.

"He's my fiancé," Winslow says, her breath reeking of vodka. "We're getting married."

Charlie coughs and her mouth drops open, but it's Tatum that gives a hard laugh. "You really are a douchebag."

"We're not..." I try to push Winslow off me, but she staggers again, and I have to hold her up. "She's drunk. And we're not engaged."

Charlie shakes her head and starts to walk away.

"Charlie."

"Who's Charlie?" Winslow asks, eyes now practically closed.

"The girl you just ruined my chances with. Where's Prescott. He said he was with you."

Her arms wrap around my neck. "Take me home, Spencer."

I know I have to. I'd never hear the end of it from my parents if I left her like this. But I clench my jaw as I watch Charlie move farther into the crowd and see Tatum hovering over her possessively. The dickhead even has the nerve to look back at me and grin triumphantly.

"Spencer," Winslow whines again. I've never

seen her like this. She's usually poised and self-controlled, worried more about what people will say about her than having fun. Which apparently she's had too much of tonight.

"I swear if you puke in my car, you're paying for the cleaning."

"I want you to clean me," she murmurs in my ear as I help her outside, fingernails dragging down my chest and snaking under my shirt. "I want your tongue to lick every dirty—"

I grab her wrist. "Not happening, Win. Ever."

"But you love me," she pouts. "We're going to get married."

I help her into my car, then buckle her seatbelt. "I care about you. Always will. But you and I will never happen."

As I shut the door, I swear I hear her giggle and say, "We'll see."

6

CHARLIE

I SHOULDN'T BE SURPRISED that Spencer left with Winslow. The woman is everything I'm not. Drop-dead gorgeous, perfect, rich. And I can't help but admit that they look good together. I reach for another beer, but before I get a single malty sip, Tatum is pulling me away from the kitchen and leading me to the dance floor.

He grins. "Wait for it, Charlotte." He points to the ceiling just as the bass drops on one of our favorite songs: "No Diggity."

I may have a penchant for vinyl records of a bygone era, but I also have a love affair with nineties R&B. Blackstreet starts blaring through the speakers and everyone starts shouting, singing along, grinding in a way that reminds me that no matter how Ivy League this group may be, we still like to back it up.

Tatum and I work the dance floor - we're terrible, but we're having fun, and really on a night where he deserves to feel like a champion for winning the game for the Tigers, that is all that matters.

"Nice moves, Hayes," Decan, one of Tatum's football friends, says in my ear, grinding up against me. The guy has always given me the creeps, so I just laugh and move away from him, closer to Tatum, who doesn't seem to notice that his friend's dark gaze is locked on me.

The dance floor parts as Tatum does his haphazard break dance moves and everyone is clapping, impressed as they should be. He's drunk, and I offer him my hand so he doesn't fall on his ass. He's so much stronger than me though, that it's me falling onto him.

His hand is on my waist, and the dancers move in on us as the song ends, a pulsing electronic beat replacing the laughter. When he looks down at me, I know he sees something he wants, but I shake my head. I love Tatum, but I don't want to kiss him.

I know that if things got physical between us, it

would ruin our friendship. And his friendship means so much.

He immediately retreats, his eyes going dark, replacing his desire with a shrug. "It's cool, Charlotte."

But it's not, he's moving through the crowd, upset. I did that to him. Me. What kind of friend am I? I weave through the crowd, reaching for his hand, and pulling him down a hallway. It's quieter and I'm grateful. I want to talk to him. I want him to hear me.

"You don't have to explain," he says. "You have your sights set on that rich fuck."

"Hey," I say, bruised for Spencer, but also for me. "You don't have to be a jerk about it."

"You know I always thought we'd end up together, Charlotte. Ever since the first day we met freshman year."

Tatum's had a lot to drink and I don't want him to say something he might regret. I shake my head. "You don't have to do —"

He cuts me off. "Let me say my piece. I thought there would be time, for us. But when I saw you with that douchebag earlier, outside your room, I knew I was too late. I thought you'd wait for me, but it looks like he got to you first."

I scoff, irritation taking hold of me. "Spencer Beckett and I aren't together if that's what you think. And secondly, if you wanted me so bad why didn't you say anything for the last three years?"

Tatum runs a hand over his neck. "Because I don't want a fling, Charlotte. If I have you, it will be for keeps."

Tears fill my eyes. Why is he doing this tonight, of all nights? I've imagined Tatum and me over the years, but he has never given me any signal to make me think he saw me anywhere but in the friend zone.

"You've been my one constant at Princeton, my shoulder to cry on. Tatum, you're my best friend. I don't want to lose that."

He smirks and I hate it, that look. It isn't him, it's not the Tatum I know and love. "Right, you wouldn't want to ruin our friendship."

"I don't." I blink, hot tears in my eyes.

"What kills me, is that you'd rather have Spencer Beckett than me."

"I don't have Spencer. He just left with Winslow Harrington. Heiress and supermodel. I don't think he's interested in me." The tone in my voice gives me away though and I know Tatum hears it.

"But you wish he were, though. That's the problem, Charlotte. If you want a guy like Princeton Fucking Charming, you'd never be happy with me."

I wipe my eyes, hating the way this night has gone down. "I love you, Tatum."

"I love you too." He drops his head, closing his eyes. "Problem is love can mean a million different things." He pulls me to his chest, kissing my forehead and I hate that I've hurt him, that he's hurt me.

It would be easier to sink against him, to let his familiar arms wrap around me and hug me in a way he's never hugged me before. It would be easy to try this out, friends-to-lovers and see if it took -- but it would be wrong, and it would be fake.

I love Tatum but not like that.

He pulls away, giving me the saddest smile a game-winning athlete has ever worn.

"What now?" I ask, hating the idea of things getting awkward between us.

He laughs. "Dammit, you really killed my vibe tonight. It was all go big or go home."

Cringing, I apologize. "I'm sorry. But don't go home. Tonight is your night. Can you go get drunk and forget about me?"

He raises his hands in the air. "A boy can dream, Charlotte Hayes, a boy can dream."

With swagger in his step, he walks away, but I know it's taking all of his strength to keep it together. I hate that I've hurt him, but I hate the idea of lying to him even more.

Still, the night is filled with way more drama than I expected.

I head out the front entrance of the house, wanting to get home to cozy PJs more than anything else. It's cold as I step outside, and the frosty air nips my nose. Christmas is going to be here before I know it, and if I want to celebrate with my family, I need a job more than I need any guy problems.

There were way too many males vying for my attention tonight. And the reason I'm a wreck is because I wasn't even torn. Yes, I hate the idea of hurting Tatum, but my heart - okay, that's not true - my *body* wants Spencer. A man so off-the-table it's embarrassing to crave more of his kisses.

He left the party with another woman after bringing me.

People have reputations for reasons.

I'm pulling on my mittens as I walk down the blustery sidewalk, wishing I had my bicycle to ride home when my attention is pulled to the bushes to my right.

"Oh God, I'm going to die… I just. I need…"

The moans get my attention, and they aren't sexual in nature - they are *painful*. "Help," the voice begs as the whimpering continues.

"Hello?" I call out, crouching to the ground. "Can you hear me?" I crawl to a body sprawled out on the grass, faint lamplight revealing that it's a woman.

"I think... I can't..." The woman closes her eyes as I reach her. She's moaning, in absolute agony, and clearly in need of help.

"I'm going to call an ambulance."

"No," she whimpers. "I just need...Oh God..."

As I reach for my phone, I realize it's Spencer's sister. The girl he was fighting with earlier.

Blond ponytail and upturned nose, but her shirt is covered in vomit and she's groaning as she curls up in a ball.

Pulling out my phone, I dial 911, knowing there is no way in hell I'm leaving this poor girl alone out here. Not when most of the campus is out partying tonight. The operator keeps me on the line as an ambulance heads our way. I know campus security could have helped, but this girl isn't simply passed out from drinking. She's clutching her stomach and writhing in pain.

When the ambulance arrives, I look around,

wishing Spencer would magically appear. Wishing anyone would appear. But the student body is partying way too hard inside posh buildings to notice a girl being helped onto a stretcher.

The medic tells me to get in with her, and I nod. "Her name is Ava," I tell them, remembering Spencer's words at the party. "Ava Beckett."

"She's lucky you called," the paramedic says as we pull away from the curb. "This girl needed a fairy godmother tonight."

I press my lips together, determined to remain calm, feeling like this night is about as far from a fairy tale as it could get.

7

SPENCER

After dropping Winslow off at her apartment, and practically prying the woman's arms off me, I sit in my car and stare out the windshield at the orange and yellow leaves that litter the streets.

Every part of me wants to go back to Tiger Inn and claim my girl. But after the stunt Winslow just pulled, I doubt Charlie will ever talk to me again. And I'm not sure why I even care. I barely even know the girl.

My phone vibrates in my pocket, and I groan when I see it's Prescott. I ignore the call, turning on the ignition, but when it buzzes again, I answer it.

"What?"

"Where are you?" Prescott growls out on the other end.

"Don't even get me started—"

"Are you with Ava?"

That gets my attention. "I saw her at the Tiger Inn a couple of hours ago. Why?"

There's a short pause. "Look, don't freak out, but—"

"What the hell happened?"

"I don't know. I just got a text from Bloomberg saying he saw her get taken away in an ambulance."

That old fear, the one that sits close to the surface, ready to consume and destroy erupts in my chest, but I manage to keep my voice unnaturally calm. "You're sure?"

"Pettit was there too. He said it was her."

"Fuck." I hang up and toss my phone on the seat beside me, then speed through the streets toward the hospital.

Memories of the night I got the call about Ethan slam into my head.

A car horn blares and wheels squeal as I go through a stop sign, but I don't slow down, not until I pull up to the emergency department, parking my Mercedes in a no-park zone and racing through the sliding glass doors.

"Ava Beckett," I demand to the receptionist. "She was brought in by ambulance. Where is she?"

"Sir, you're going to have to——"

"She's my sister, and unless you want a lawsuit slapped on your——"

"Spencer." Charlie is walking toward me frowning, and it takes me a second to register that it's her.

"What are you doing here?"

"I'm the one who found Ava." She motions me away from the receptionist who looks ready to call security on me. "I came in the ambulance with her."

"Where is she? Is she okay?" I can hear the panic in my voice.

"A doctor is with her now. They hooked her up to an IV and are running some tests. But I think she'll be fine. She was pretty drunk."

I lean against the cold wall and drag my hands over my face, realizing that a cold sweat has broken out over my forehead.

"Are *you* all right?" She places a hand on my arm.

"Yeah," I lie, straightening, not wanting her to see the wreck I am right now. "Thanks for helping her."

She nods. "I was just going to get a coffee. Do you want one?"

"You don't have to stay."

"I know, I just..." She wraps her arms around herself. "I want to make sure she's all right. I can go if you want—"

"No." I force a smile. "I'd appreciate a coffee."

She nods before disappearing down the hall toward the cafeteria.

"Mr. Beckett?" the receptionist says a few minutes later, the scowl still on her face when she addresses me. "You can go back now."

I find my sister on a gurney, an IV in her arm, mascara staining her pale cheeks. She whimpers when she sees me and covers her face with her hands. "Who told you I was here?"

"Prescott." I sit on a plastic chair beside the bed.

"He knows too?" she groans.

"Pretty sure half the campus is aware of you leaving in an ambulance." Which means our parents will know soon enough as well. "What the hell were you thinking?"

"I was just having fun."

"And this..." I lift my hands and look around. "This is your idea of fun?"

"Stop judging me. I've heard stories about you—"

"That's different."

"Why? Because you're the great Princeton Charming? Give me a break, Spencer. You're just as messed up as I am."

"Never said I wasn't." I take her hand and sigh.

"God, we're a pair aren't we?" she says. "You screwing your way through half the campus, me trying to drink away the empty hole in my chest."

"I haven't screwed half the campus," I mutter. "And even if I had I really don't need my little sister talking about it."

"Right, because Becketts don't talk about anything real. No wonder Ethan drove his car off that cliff."

Her words hit me like a punch to the gut.

"It was an accident," I say, a little too forcefully, causing Ava's brows to rise, but then she shakes her head and gives me a look filled with pity.

"Believe whatever makes you sleep at night."

"You weren't even there."

She sighs and looks away. "He called me that night. He sounded..."

I pull my hand away. "He was fucked up on drugs. Ethan loved life. He wouldn't..." But there's that nagging voice in the back of my head that has always questioned if it really was an accident.

Lies.

Deceit.

They follow my damn family around like a plague.

Ava glances over my shoulder and I follow her gaze. Charlie stands there, chewing on her bottom lip, holding two coffee cups, and I wonder how much of our conversation she heard.

"You're still here?" Ava says giving Charlie a grateful smile. "Thank you again for helping me. Charlie, this is my brother—"

"Yeah, we've met," Charlie says, handing me a coffee.

"Of course you have," Ava mutters with a small eye roll. "It's hard to make friends when my brother has screwed—"

"Ava," I warn.

She just shrugs, and I see Charlie frown.

"So, um, I..." Charlie fidgets with her coffee cup.

God, I want to pull the girl into my arms. *Mine*, that alpha part of my brain demands with a ferocity I've never felt before.

I'm aware of the silence, but for all my usual charm, I'm not sure what to say.

"I just..." Charlie continues, her gaze focused on

Ava. "I wanted to make sure you were all right before I go."

"You're so sweet. And cute." Ava grins at me like she knows a secret. "Isn't she cute, Spence?"

Cute? No. The girl is beautiful. Gorgeous even. Not in the porcelain way like Winslow, but because of her tiny flaws.

"Yeah," I breathe out.

"Well..." Charlie's cheeks turn red and she still doesn't meet my gaze. "I should go."

"Do you have a ride home?" I ask.

"I'll get an Uber."

"Spence can drive you," Ava offers quickly, a hint of a smile on her lips, and a spark of mischief in her eyes. "I'll be here for at least a few more hours."

I glance back at Charlie, who doesn't look convinced. But then why would she trust me? And I still don't know what's up with her and Tatum. But I'm also not about to let her take an Uber home when she just spent her entire night taking care of my drunk ass little sister.

"Let's go." I stand, about to take her hand, then stopping myself.

"Really, it's fine, I'll just—"

"I'm driving you home." I give her a look,

begging her to argue, because I'd rather hear her smart mouth than silence, but she just nods.

I kiss Ava's forehead and mutter, "You're not off the hook. When I get back, we're going to talk about this."

"Or what? You going to tell Mom and Dad?" I hear the hurt in her voice, the need and desire to have parents who actually gave a shit that their daughter is spiraling.

"I'll be back." I squeeze her hand, then lead Charlie out toward where I parked my car. Thankfully it hasn't been towed.

The silence between us is deafening as I drive her back to her dorm.

"Winslow and I aren't—"

"It's none of my business," she says, gaze focused anywhere but on me.

"She's an old family friend."

"So you've never slept with her?"

"I don't sleep with people, Charlie, I fuck them. And yes, Winslow and I have a history. But that's all it is, history."

"Except that she thinks you're engaged."

"If our parents had their way, we would be. She was drunk tonight, and I drove her home. That's it. And you seemed to be occupied." Even I hear the jealousy that creeps into my voice. "That guy, Tatum...he likes you."

She runs her palms over her thighs. "Tatum and I are just friends."

"Good." I take her hand.

"Spencer, I..." She swallows. "I can't do this."

"Why not?"

She gives a small laugh. "Because I don't just *fuck*. That's not me. I want..."

I pull over to the curb in front of her dorm. "What do you want? Tell me." Right now I'm ready to give her almost anything.

"I want things someone like you could never give me."

I wince at the harsh reality of her words, knowing she's probably right.

"Try me."

"Spencer—"

"Charlie," I say, taking her chin between my fingers and turning her face toward me. "I like you."

She grunts. "You want to fuck—"

"Before you finish that sentence, I'll admit I do. I want you bad. From the first time I laid eyes on you, I wanted to kiss you, to bury myself inside of you and hear you call out my name. So yeah, I want to fuck you. But I'm willing to compromise."

"How romantic." She rolls her eyes at me.

"Is that what you want? Romance?"

"No. Yes." She shakes her head. "Maybe. I don't know. I'm too busy to even think about what I want."

I frown, knowing what it's like to live under the expectations of others, and I wonder who she's living for. Her parents?

"You're a challenge, Charlie Hayes. I like that." I like it a lot. Like her a lot.

"I'm not trying to be. We just...we're not right for each other. I don't fit in your world."

"But I bet I would fit perfectly *in* you," I tease, hoping to ease some of the tension between us.

She laughs. "God, you really are corny."

"Only with you, babe." I twine my fingers in hers, and she glances down at where our flesh meets. "Give me a chance. At least one more date. I can't have this blemish on my record."

"A blemish, huh?" She shakes her head. "Trust me. You've gotten farther than most guys. Think of it as a win."

"Until I'm buried inside you, Charlie, everything else is a loss." I press my hand to her cheek, my thumb running over the orange and black stripes. "Our face paint is looking pretty bad. You sure you don't want me to come upstairs and help clean you up?"

Charlie lifts her eyebrows, pink tongue darting over her lips. "You want to take a shower with me, Spencer?"

"It would be romantic, just like you want."

"Right, I can just picture it now," she says playfully. She drops her voice, taking on a sultry tone. Her bright eyes though, tell me this is all a tease. "You and me, stripped down in the dorm room bathroom, my caddy of shampoo and body wash at our heels. A plastic curtain. Fluorescent lighting. Super romantic."

I laugh, not having met a woman like her before. Down to earth. Real. Like a girl-next-door, but so hot it makes my balls ache. "You like playing hard to get?"

She chuckles, smirking. Stepping out of the car. "What can I say? I liked to be chased."

"Good."

"Yeah?" she asks, leaning in the car, hand on the door.

I shake my head. "Charlotte Hayes, you're not gonna be the one who got away."

8

CHARLIE

I TEXT Daphne after Spencer drops me off wondering where my crazy roommate is sleeping tonight, or rather who with. I can't help but feel somewhat responsible for her. She sends me a string of emojis letting me know she's good. I think. I'm not exactly sure what three eggplants, a unicorn, and a boat mean, but I think it's her way of telling she's finally hooking up with the rowing crew she's been crushing on for months.

More power to her.

Me? Forever the virgin, who's too scared to ever take the risk and give myself to someone.

I wash my face, get in pajamas, and run my fingers over my record collection, looking for the perfect album to put me to sleep. The night was exhausting in so many ways, but also, there's this tingling sense of hope that runs over me.

Maybe it's crazy to think that Spencer might really want the chase with me, that maybe he isn't all talk.

That kiss was real.

Really powerful.

At least for me. Or maybe it's all part of his charm. The man has a reputation for a reason.

My phone buzzes. I frown when I see a text from my mom. It's nearly midnight here, she should be sleeping, but I know she's been having more and more trouble lately managing her pain.

Mom: Dad just told me Tatum won the game! Go Tigers!

I smile, feeling so lucky to have parents who are so invested in my life.

Me: It was pretty epic. He earned bragging rights for sure.

My thumbs hover over the keypad. She has enough on her mind that I don't want to burden her with my boy trouble, and job problems. I still haven't told them that I was fired. She and Dad aren't in a place to help me with any of them anyway.

Me: Miss you.

Mom: Miss you more, sweetpea. Just had Dad pull out Christmas decorations. Will wait to do the tree until you get home.

Hot tears fill my eyes and I wipe them away. How am I going to get back home when my checking account is in such a sorry state?

Me: Can't wait. The countdown is on :)

Mom: 22 days until your break!

I swallow. Okay, the countdown is literally on.

Me: G2G. XOXO

I set down my phone, wishing things were easier. Spencer and Winslow and Tatum and poor Ava. It was a complicated blur of a night. I pull out The Partridge Family Christmas Album feeling a strong tug of nostalgia for home. I take the record out of the sleeve and place it on the platter, and set the tone arm down. The familiar sounds of Christmas fill my room, and I get in bed, hoping for sweet sleep.

I WAKE to my phone buzzing again. My first thought is something's happened with Mom, but when I look at the incoming text, I see it's Jill. We met last year because the two of us were both looking for extra jobs on the bulletin board outside the student center. We bonded over the fact we are both work-study students who are also thrift store junkies. Clichéd, maybe. Frugal - for sure. After scouring the racks at the Goodwill together, we decided anytime we needed a shift covered on campus we'd have one another's backs.

She still doesn't know I lost my gig last week. I've been a waitress for campus events for two years and she's been a janitor. Both jobs have their perks. She has more job security since she works alone. Meaning no chance of losing her paycheck over tossing champagne in someone's face.

Jill: You up for it? It's a 4 hour shift.

Me: Yes. Please!!!!!!

Jill: LOL. Simmer down. You strapped for cash?

Me: Aren't I always?

Jill: Touché. I'll drop off the keys if that's cool?

Later, after Jill's brought me the keys and given me the details, I dig through my drawers for something to wear. I settle on ripped boyfriend jeans, Converse, and an oversized black sweater, figuring I don't need to make a fashion statement this afternoon. I tie a red bandana in my hair and call it good.

As I'm about to leave, Daphne struts in. I look at the clock. Eleven am. She is carrying two cups of coffee, however, and hands me one.

"Where are you going?" she asks, she's wearing a guy's hoodie and it reaches her mid-thigh, right where her boots end. Some people may call this the walk of shame, but Daphne owns it.

"I'm going to cover Jill's shift."

"Boo!" Daphne pouts before taking a sip of her coffee.

"Thanks for this," I say, lifting the cup to cheers her. "I take it the rowing team showed you a good time?"

"They were no Princeton Charming, but yeah, we had fun." She grins, and I shake my head.

"Spencer and I are not a thing, so don't get any ideas in your head."

"You're not interested?"

"No way. He's so not my type."

"I wish you didn't have to work," she says.

I groan. "You're telling me, sweetheart."

"I miss you though," she says. "We haven't hung out in ages. I was hoping we could chill today."

She's always finding something to keep her busy. Sometimes though, I worry about her. She keeps a pretty positive outlook most of the time, but I've seen her get down, missing class and needing to regroup at home for a few weeks.

"Rain check?" I pull my tote bag over my shoulder, keys in hand. Before I can go, though, there is a knock on the door. Frowning, I pull it open.

Standing there with a bouquet of red roses is Spencer Beckett.

"What's this?" I ask.

He offers me the roses. "It's me thanking you for everything last night."

I lift my eyebrows and take the flowers. "This isn't necessary."

"I thought you asked for romance."

I laugh. "I'm more practical than this. I'd rather have a rose bush than a bouquet."

"And what would you do with a rose bush, Charlotte Hayes?" he asks.

Twisting my lips, I shrug. "Plant it. It would last longer than these." I bring the bouquet to my nose and inhale. The sweet scent of flowers fills my nostrils and I sigh. These are some really gorgeous roses.

"Just say thank you," he says, his signature smile

making my heart beat fast. "It's the polite thing to do."

"Where are my manners?" I tease, pressing a hand to my chest. "Thank you, Princeton Charming. For this grand gesture meant to sweep me off my feet."

"You are trouble, you know that?"

I nod. "I do."

Daphne interjects, taking the roses from me. "I'll put these in water. And don't you have a job to get to?" she asks me pointedly. I see she is trying to help me get away from Spencer, and I appreciate it.

But I also realize my earlier comments about him to her weren't exactly honest. Flirting with Spencer is fun. Really fun. And I don't want it to end.

"A job?" he asks. "I thought—"

I cut him off. "I'm covering a friend's shift."

"I was hoping we could go out today, maybe ice skate, something Christmassy. Something *romantic*."

"Sorry to be a heartbreaker, but I've got work to do. And the sooner I start cleaning the library, the sooner I will be done."

"I can help," he says. "Two people are better than one, right?"

"Ha. Campus royalty can't be seen with

commoners. Besides, do you even know how to run a vacuum cleaner?"

His eyes go wide, and he laughs. "I'm a quick learner." I start to shake my head, but he persists. "Please. Let me help. I'm trying to thank you for helping Ava last night. Let me be the good guy."

"As opposed to?"

"Whatever it is you think I am."

My lips twitch. Dusting shelves would be a lot more fun with Spencer Beckett at my side. I shrug, feigning nonchalance. Inside my heart pounds. "Fine."

"Fine?"

"Yeah, fine." I press a hand to his chest, his face lights up with a smile, and I walk past him into the hallway. "You wanna come help me clean, I'm not going to stop you."

<hr />

THE LAW LIBRARY is closed on Sundays, so it's just Spencer and me. I flick on some lights and turn to my work-buddy.

"You up for this?" I ask, trying hard to control the grin that tugs at my lips.

"It's like you don't think I know what it means to work up a sweat."

"Do you?"

He smirks, closing the distance between us. "That's what I've been trying to tell you, Charlie. I know all about working up a sweat."

I laugh. "I think we're discussing two very different types of work."

He lifts an eyebrow. "I wouldn't mind watching you show me how it's done. This work of yours."

I laugh, stepping toward the supply closet. "You just want to see me bend over as I wield a broom."

"Fair enough." He joins me in the closet, and I feel the electricity between us rise. "So, what do you want me to do?"

Kiss me. The thought comes out of nowhere. I swallow hard. "I...uh...you should..."

He leans closer, that cocky smirk playing on his lips. "I should what, Charlie?"

It's terrible how much I want him. His kiss. His touch. The way he looks at me, like he's ready to devour every inch of my body, makes my core clench in need. I'd let him -- consume me. In this moment if he asked, hell if he just took, I'd give in, unable to resist.

His breathing is ragged, matching my own, but

he doesn't kiss me, he just presses his forehead to mine and keeps his hands at his side.

"We better get to work." His warm breath tickles my lips. "Because once I get you out of here, you're all mine tonight."

As much of a cliché as it is, I want to be his, even if it's just for one night.

"I hope you don't think just cause you're helping me clean I'm going to have sex with you. Maybe that's the way it works with your other girls, but I'm not them."

He laughs. "Trust me, Charlie, one thing I've come to realize is that you're nothing like anyone I've ever met before. And this—" He takes the broom from my hand. "Is all new to me too. But I'll make you a bet." He's grinning at me, like whatever he's about to propose, he's already won.

"What kind of a bet?"

He moves toward me, and I take a couple steps back until my ass hits the shelves. His gaze rakes over me, lust and need burning in his eyes. "By the end of today, it'll be you begging to be in my bed."

"I don't beg."

"Not yet." He kisses the tip of my nose, then winks. "But you will."

He chuckles and moves out of the room, broom

in hand, and I'm left wondering if making bets with Princeton Charming may just be the way I can get what I want. Him.

9

SPENCER

SPENDING the day cleaning with Charlie proves to be more difficult than I expected, mostly because my balls ache like a motherfucker from watching that sweet little ass bending over constantly.

But more than that, the girl is quick, and not just her snarky little comments meant to keep me at arm's length. She's smart. And funny. And by the time we're putting the cleaning supplies back in the supply closet I'm starting to wonder if this isn't just about the conquest. If maybe it's more. More than I'm willing to consider right now.

"So, Charming," she says as she locks up. "You survived a day with the commoners."

I grunt. "You act like I've never worked before."

"Have you? I figure someone like you has a cushiony trust fund he can tap into whenever he needs a new Rolex or—"

I spin her around, hands on her waist, and pull her toward me. "You like to put people in boxes."

"Doesn't everyone?" Her palms are on my chest, ready to push me away, but she doesn't. "Honestly, Spencer. What do you see when you look at me? A scholarship student from a blue collar family, who'll never belong in your world."

"Last I checked, there's only one world we live in. And those are just things, Charlie. Money—"

"Or lack of."

I chuckle. "Sure. But it doesn't make us who we are."

"So you're saying you wouldn't care if you woke up tomorrow and were broke."

"I didn't say that."

She laughs. "Right."

"So you don't like rich people." My arms are still around her, and there's no way I'm moving unless she pushes me away.

"No, it's not that..." She chews on her bottom lip and frowns.

"Then what? You're here at Princeton. One of

the top schools in the country. When you graduate, you can't tell me you won't jump at the chance to make some good coin."

"Of course not, but I want to make money so I can..." She starts to pull away.

"Not so fast." I spread my fingers at her lower back and feel her shiver against me. "Tell me."

"You have money, so you don't have to worry about getting sick, paying for bills, watching people you love suffer..."

"Hate to break it to you, but being rich doesn't mean we don't get sick."

"See. That right there. You don't get it. Sure, you get sick, but you go to the top hospitals, have the best doctors. You don't have to worry about re-mortgaging your house to pay for life-saving treatments."

I frown down at her. "You have someone who's sick?"

She hesitates before answering. "My mom. She was diagnosed with Multiple Sclerosis when I was nine. It wasn't bad at first, but..."

"I'm sorry." I cup her jaw, seeing the pain in her eyes, and hell if I don't want to take it away.

"It's been hard watching her lose her ability to

do the things she once did. And my dad, God, he works so hard, trying to take care of her, and working to pay the bills. It's just not fair. How some people can have so much, and others..." She swipes her fingers under her eyes. "I'm not sure why I told you that."

"Because I asked." I press my lips against her forehead. "I want to know about you."

She grunts. "Why? So you can feel better about yourself—"

"There's that chip again."

She shrugs. "Maybe. But it's who I am. I have to work hard just to keep my head above water. That's why I need this job, why I needed that waitressing job."

"I won't make the mistake of offering you money again. But..." I grin down at her, hoping to lighten the mood. "I can see about getting you a job at The Blue Point Grill. The owner owes me a favor."

"I don't need your help—"

"You kind of do. And since I'm the one responsible for screwing up your other gig, I'd like to do something."

Her lips pinch together, and I can practically see the wheels turning in her head.

"You don't owe me anything," I say, getting the feeling that's what she's worried about.

She sighs. "I'll find my own job."

I want to argue with her, but I know it's pointless. Instead, I change the subject. "So, how about that date?"

She glances down at her baggy sweater and jeans. "I'm not really dressed to go out. I should go back to the dorm and change."

"Or you can come back to my place and I'll order Chinese."

"Your place, huh?" Her lips purse again, and I can see her mulling over the option. "I guess I wouldn't mind seeing where royalty lives. Is there a drawbridge and moat?"

I chuckle. "Hardly. But every once in a while a fire-breathing dragon comes by."

"Really?" A smile lights up her face.

"I'm serious. You haven't met my mother yet. But you'll understand when you do."

She tenses slightly, and I wonder if I've gone too far. The words slipped out. But I know they didn't come from nowhere. I took enough psych classes in undergrad to know the subconscious is more powerful than we give it credit for. And I'm pretty sure mine has marked this girl...and not just for a quick fling.

It's scary as hell, but even though I feel like I'm barrelling down a hill in a cart with no brakes, I'm enjoying the fucking ride, and I don't want it to stop.

10

CHARLIE

SPENCER'S PLACE may not be a castle, but it's unlike anything I've ever seen before. Decorated in whites and grays, it looks more like an apartment out of Better Homes, than something a college guy would live in. Except of course, for the large pool table situated in the center of the living room, and the enormous plasma TV mounted above a gas fireplace.

"God, you really are rich."

"Don't hold it against me." He smirks.

"Let me guess, you have a maid to clean up after you?"

He shrugs. "She only comes once a week."

"Oh my God." I groan. "This is..."

"You don't like it?"

"It's gorgeous. And the rent is probably double what I pay in a year for my dorm room."

"I wouldn't know, my parents own the building."

"Of course they do." He's Princeton Charming, after all, heir to one of the wealthiest families in the state.

"You think I'm a jackass, don't you? Because of all this? And you're probably right. But I have money of my own."

"That you've actually worked for?"

He winces. "You going to hold it against me for having a small trust fund?"

"Small, huh?"

His shoulders lift and fall.

I can't even imagine what type of money he's talking about, and I don't want to know.

"Money comes and goes," I say.

"I take care of what's mine," he says, striding toward me, a silent message in his eyes. *He wants to own me.*

And there's a part of me that wants it too. But it goes against everything I believe in, every women's lib course that I've ever been a part of.

"You can't own people." I jut my chin up at him.

"I didn't say I could."

"But you implied—"

He takes my face in his hands and lets out a heavy breath. "I'm starting to think you like arguing."

"I am pre-law."

A deep rumble of laughter comes from his chest. "And you'll make a damn good lawyer one day."

I'm acutely aware of the fact that for most of the day I've had Spencer's undivided attention. As he moves closer to me, I am ready for that kiss he's been teasing for hours. But my stomach rumbles. Loudly. And he chuckles, shaking his head. "You're really good at putting off the inevitable, Charlie."

I exhale, pressing my hands to my belly. "I haven't eaten all day."

"Let's fix that then, shall we?" Spencer pulls out his phone as we walk toward the kitchen. Granite counters, stainless steel, and when he opens the fridge to grab drinks, all it is stocked with are beverages.

"Not a cook?"

"Nope," he laughs. Then he turns his phone toward me. "I'll place an order for Chinese. Have any favorites?"

SOON ENOUGH WE have containers of take-out sprawled around his kitchen island. He sits on a bar stool and I've hitched myself up on the counter. The fact that he's sitting right in front of me sends a warm burst of desire through me. It would take no time at all to spread my knees, to move between me, to give me the one thing I've always been too nervous to take.

Chopsticks in hand, we inhale dinner. Noodles and potstickers and orange chicken. "A girl with an appetite," he says. "God, I'm learning so much about you today."

"Girls you usually date prefer salad and—"

He cuts me off. "I don't want to talk about any other girls tonight, understood?"

I nod, licking my lips. When he gets bossy, it sends a shiver over my spine. "I understand. But don't get too controlling, Spencer Beckett. I won't call you Sir, if that's where you think this is headed."

His lips twitch and he sets down the box of Chinese. He sets his hands on my knees and I press my lips together. This is going to happen.

"Charlie, you're really a piece of work, you know that?"

"I didn't, actually."

"Well, you are. And I like it."

"The challenge?"

He shakes his head. "The chase."

I swallow as he stands, plucking the chopsticks from my fingers, wrapping his arms around my waist. "I think you won the bet," I manage to eek out.

He tucks a loose strand of hair behind my ear, lifting my chin. "I told you I never lose."

"I'm starting to understand why."

He kisses me then, his mouth dipping to mine, his hands firm on my hips. He inches me closer to the edge of the counter and my legs wrap around his torso. This isn't logical, methodical Charlotte. This is me, letting my emotions, my body lead me. I'll go anywhere tonight.

His lips part and his tongue finds mine and I sink into that kiss, into him. He lifts me from the counter, and I know it's right. Him and me in this moment.

I kiss him back with all the pent-up sexual energy I've never let loose. Wrapping my legs around his waist, I don't fight it. I want to be his, even if it's just for tonight.

Up the stairs, we go. Panting for breath. Laughing.

"I'm finally going to have you, Charlie," he growls against my neck, kicking the door to his bedroom open. "You're mine, now."

My arms are around his neck and he carries me as if I'm weightless. It's the same way my heart feels right now. Like I am floating.

In his room the lights are low, the sun has begun to set, sending brilliant pinks and purples through his windows. He presses a switch, blackout shades drop. The moment turns even more intimate as he places me on his enormous bed.

"You look beautiful," he says, leaning down, his arms on either side of me.

I smirk, pressing a hand to my forehead. "In these ratty clothes? Yeah, a real hottie."

"Don't do that."

"Getting bossy again, are you?"

"About this, yes." He lowers my hand. "You are beautiful Charlie. So fucking beautiful."

My cheeks heat up, my core awake. "You make me nervous."

"Good. It'll keep you on your toes."

I close my eyes as he kisses my neck, as his hands run up my body, under my sweater. I inhale.

"You want this?" he asks.

"I need this," I confess.

My words cause him to groan in pleasure as he runs his hands over my breasts, under my back. Unhooking my bra with such a seamless, fluid motion, I am reminded just how insane it is to be here, with him. Our mouths collide, the kisses intensifying as he massages my breasts.

My back arches and I press a hand to his strong, solid chest. I want him to be naked, against me. Inside me. I want my first time to be with Spencer Beckett and I want it now.

He tugs off his shirt and my fingers run over his corded muscles, his ladder of abs -- I breathe in his masculinity, feeling intoxicated with his strength. He unbuttons my jeans, pulls them off. My panties are white, and my body has never been touched, never looked at, not the way he looks at me now. A flutter of innocence washes over me.

"I want to taste you, Charlie." He looks at me

solemnly, with a seriousness that tells me his want for me is no joke.

"God," I squeak out as he hooks the waistband of my panties with his thumbs, as he drags me to the edge of the bed, as he kneels before me, ready to make my pussy his.

I don't care if he's gone down on half the campus because right now his hands are on my thighs, spreading them apart. Right now his mouth plants kisses against my skin and all that matters is this.

His mouth is on me, His tongue swiping over my slick entrance. I'm wet for him and he knows it and when he looks up, into my eyes, I know he likes it.

"God, your pussy is so fucking sweet."

I moan, half incredulous, half enamored, entirely melting for this man. He spreads my knees, his tongue running up and down my slit. I whimper as his mouth devours me, sucking against my tender folds with increasing need. His hands are warm, and they squeeze my ass, dragging me closer to his willing mouth.

"Oh Spence," I moan, covering my face as a spell is cast over me. My body is spinning out of my control, inching toward a release only he can give.

There is no denying that he knows how to work my body into submission. If he wants me to call him Sir, right now I would.

His fingers find my entrance, he eases one, then two inside me and I bite my lip, pleasure rocking through me. "You're so tight, Charlie. So fucking tight."

"It's because I've never slept with someone," I murmur as his tongue swirls against my tender clit.

He stops. The licking and sucking and delicate grind of his fingers against my G-spot.

"You're a virgin?" His hand is still tight against my pussy and I don't want him to move it. His eyes though are dark as he meets my gaze.

"I am," I tell him, panting with want. I reach for his hand, eager for him to make me come.

"Charlie, I didn't know."

"That's okay. I want this. You. Don't stop."

He removes his hand, pulling himself up on the bed, towering over me. I feel the thickness of his aching cock as he cradles me in his arm, brushing the hair from my face, looking deep into my eyes.

"I can't fuck a virgin like this."

"Like what?" I ask, not wanting this to end. "Today *has* been romantic. Roses. And Chinese and—"

He laughs. "And cleaning a library. Mops and brooms are very sexy." He kisses my nose. "No wonder you were such a tease. My little Charlie Hayes is a virgin."

It's not the first time today that he's called me his.

"You laying claim to me?" I ask, wrapping my legs around him. Pinning him to me. He's not leaving me before he makes me come.

"I think I am."

"Good," I say. "Then don't stop."

"I can't have your first time be like this."

"But I may never get another chance to lose my virginity to the infamous Princeton Charming."

He shakes his head, kissing my jaw, my collarbone, my breasts, my belly. He slides down to the floor. "Oh, you'll get a chance all right. Tonight, though, you're the only one who is getting off."

I pout as his mouth begins to work my pussy all over again. "That's not fair."

"Says who?" he asks as his fingers slide into my wanting pussy. "From where I'm kneeling, this is more than fair. This is—"

But my moans cut him off. "Oh, Spence, oh, oh, yes, yes..." My body pulses with heat as he drops his mouth to me and begins to suck me off as I come, calling his name.

He bet that by the end of the day I'd be begging to get in his bed. He was certainly right about that. It makes me wonder as my back arches and my fingers run through his thick hair, just what else Spencer Beckett might be right about.

11

SPENCER

WE DON'T LEAVE my bed for hours. Her sweet pussy is so happy, and there is the most satisfied smile on her face that has me grinning like a goddamn fool. We tease and kiss and pinch and purr. I can't think of when I've ever had foreplay like this. That lasts hours, where the climax consists of a woman tucked against my chest. Hell, my pants are still on.

And it was the best night I've had in a long ass time. In forever.

Being with Charlie is like floating away from my current reality. She lives somewhere else. Somewhere that is more real and more sincere.

"I need music to fall asleep," she whispers, her hand on my chest.

"Oh, so you plan on spending the night?" I tease, reaching for my phone.

"You're so bad," she says, plucking my nipple.

"Ouch," I say, taking her hand in mine, kissing her fingers. "Here, you pick what we're listening to."

I open my music app for her and she begins scrolling through my playlists. I don't think she realizes just how unprecedented this is. I never, ever hand over my phone to a woman. But Charlie is different. It's like I want her to see me, all of me. I want to know what she might do with that information.

"Did you stalk me or something?" she asks, propping her chin on her hand, looking up at me.

"What do you mean?"

"Like, our music tastes are eerily similar."

"Really? I heard you had a thing for 90s R & B."

She lifts her eyebrows. "So you were stalking."

"Prescott might have mentioned something about your dance moves after I left the party."

She bites back a smile. "Okay well, yes, Tatum and I have a thing for old school music, but it's not my first love." She turns my phone screen toward me. The playlist is called Songs For When I'm Lonely. "You made this?"

I laugh, groaning. "Shit, I forgot about that one."

"Yeah right," she says, pulling the songs up. "It says the last time you played this list was two days ago."

"Fucking technology, revealing all my secrets."

"I think it's sexy," she says as The Beatles' "Eleanor Rigby," begins to play. "I should really buy this album. It's a good one."

I push my insecurities down as the familiar music washes over us. *Ah, look at all the lonely people.* I swallow, my eyes meeting Charlie's. I want her to see me, the way no one else ever does. I may be the goddamn golden boy on campus, but my life is not as effortless as it might appear. So much of it is a game, a show. And I wonder if Charlie sees a glimpse of that as the sad music fills my room. She doesn't say a word, but she doesn't need to, the music says it for us.

Charlie sets my phone on the bedside table, and I pull up the duvet over her shoulders, over mine. And wrap my arms around the most unlikely woman I've ever brought to my bed. She fits here, next to me.

But I know that the rest of my life is a different puzzle. I can't for the life of me imagine her fitting in with my parents, my friends, my future.

I kiss her soft skin as she nestles against my chest, her bare ass the most tempting thing I've ever denied myself. I don't need any more tonight. Having her in my arms is more than enough - for now.

CHARLIE

"So, are you dating him?" Jill asks, sitting across from me at the coffee shop, a mischievous grin tugging at her lips as she tries to pry information out of me.

I shrug, my heart fluttering with nerves every time I think about Spencer and our one night together. "I don't think he actually dates."

And I really have no clue what Spencer is thinking, or if he's even thinking about me at all. I've only seen him in passing and from a distance since he drove me back to my dorm three days ago. He's sent texts, and we've had a dozen flirty phone calls, but he hasn't mentioned seeing me again.

Maybe I scared him off with the whole virgin

thing. I take a sip of my spiced pumpkin latte and try not to let it bother me.

He's just a guy, Charlotte, I remind myself.

"But you had sex?" Jill asks a little too loudly, causing a few heads to turn.

"No. We just...did other things."

She shakes her head. "You want me to believe you spent the whole night with the infamous Princeton Charming and you didn't bang him?"

"He was a gentleman." And he was. But her words have all sorts of insecurities floating around in my head. Maybe I shouldn't have told him I was a virgin. But then, if this is the way he's going to treat me, maybe it's for the best that I didn't have sex with him.

"Hey beautiful," a deep voice says against my ear, and for a split second, I think it's Spencer until Prescott moves around me and pulls up a chair, straddling it beside me.

"Uh, hi. What are you doing here?" I glance around wondering if Spencer is with him.

"Getting coffee. Just like everyone else." He takes a sip from the white paper cup, then smiles at Jill. "You going to introduce me to your friend?"

"I'm Jill," she offers before I can say anything, holding out her hand and giving him her best smile.

"And you're Prescott Addington. I read your paper on human rights and immigration law."

He grunts. "Why? Were you having trouble sleeping?"

"It was really good. I disagree with you on—"

"That looks delicious," Prescott interrupts, tearing off a piece of Jill's half-eaten chocolate croissant and popping it in his mouth. "You mind grabbing me one?" He pulls out a twenty from his wallet and places it on the table in front of Jill, then asks me, "You want anything, Hayes?"

I shake my head, frowning at him.

When Jill stands and walks to the end of the long line, I turn on him, "She's not your servant."

He chuckles. "Unless you want to listen to her drone on about the 1951 Geneva convention, or whether prisoners should have the right to vote, I did you a favor." He leans back and gives me a cocky grin. "And I came over to talk to you."

"About what?" Suspicion has me pursing my lips at him.

"Tell me Beckett's full of shit. That you didn't let that dickhead into your pants."

I'm pretty sure my face goes white, because I swear I feel all the blood leave me, and Prescott just shakes his head.

"Damn, you did. Thought you were smarter than that, Hayes."

"Spencer told you that we..." I swallow over the lump that's formed in my throat. "He said we had sex?"

Prescott shrugs. "Doesn't matter anyway. You can tell the douchebag he still lost the bet."

Don't ask, don't ask, don't ask, my brain screams, but I ask anyway, "What bet?"

"Shit." His grin broadens, and I can tell he's enjoying this. "I shouldn't have said that."

"But you did, which means you wanted me to know."

He chuckles and pushes his chair back. "You're a smart girl, Hayes. But you're not in the same league as Spencer Beckett. You need to watch your back."

"Is that a threat?"

"Nah, just a warning." He winks before walking away.

"Where'd he go?" Jill returns a couple minutes later with a pastry, and she looks put out that the asshole is gone.

I roll my eyes at her. "I need to get to class."

"But it doesn't start for another forty minutes

and you still haven't given me any details about your night—"

"Because nothing happened, and nothing will happen. It was a lapse of judgment." I push my chair back and stand, grabbing my bag.

"I swear, you're holding onto that V-card with a white-knuckled grip."

My phone rings. "I need to take this," I say when I see my dad's number on the screen. "Hey, Dad." I walk out of the coffee shop, shivering as a cold wind blows around me.

"Hey baby girl." He sounds tired. "How are you doing?"

"Good. Just heading to class."

There's a long silence on the other end.

"Everything okay, Dad?"

I hear him swallow hard. "If you haven't cashed that check I gave you, I was hoping you could hold off."

"Yeah. Of course." I wasn't planning on cashing the hundred dollars that he gave me at Thanksgiving anyway. "What's going on?"

"Money is just a bit tight right now."

"Is Mom okay?"

More silence.

"Dad?"

He sighs. "She's had one of her flare-ups."

I stop walking and try to hold back the emotions that creep into my chest, wanting to choke me. Every time she has one of these attacks she always loses another piece of herself. The last one put her in a wheelchair, unable to use her legs.

"I'll come home—"

"No, sweetheart. There's nothing you can do here."

"But—"

"Charlie. I've got things under control. Just keep flying, baby girl."

I feel tears prick my eyes, knowing I can't tell him that I lost my job. That sometimes I question why I'm even here, struggling to keep my grades up, dealing with inconsequential drama like Spencer Beckett, when I should be home taking care of my mom.

Feeling numb, I head to my Advanced Legal Topics class, wondering how today could possibly get worse until I see Spencer standing at the entrance of the building I'm heading toward, Winslow standing with him, her lean body practically infused with his.

My heart sinks like a stone in my gut.

"Friends my ass," I mutter under my breath,

knowing if I'm going to get to my damn class I'm going to have to walk straight past them.

"Hey, Charlotte." Tatum is running toward me, a big, goofy grin on his face when he catches up. "Didn't you hear me calling you?"

"No. Sorry." Obviously our little disagreement from the weekend is forgotten, or he's choosing to act like it didn't happen. "I've got a lot on my mind."

I turn to him, mostly so I don't have to see Spencer and Winslow together.

"Are we still on for this afternoon?" Tatum asks.

"This afternoon?"

"You forgot." He sighs. "You said you wanted to try that new Thai restaurant."

"Right." I pull my bottom lip between my teeth. That was before I lost my job. When I actually had a few extra dollars to eat out. Now all I have is a rapidly decreasing bank account and a plane ticket that still needs to be bought. "Do you think we could go another time? I have a lot of studying to do."

"Is this because of Beckett? Is he already controlling who you can hang out with?"

"No." I shake my head. "And Spencer and I aren't...anything."

"I don't know about that," a familiar voice says before an arm drapes around my shoulder possessively.

Spencer. I think I forget to breathe.

It takes me a second to remember that I'm angry at him. I want to shrug off his arm, but I also don't want to give Tatum any more reason to strike out at him. And the way his face has turned a shade of red and his fingers form into fists, I know it's a real possibility.

I glance up at Spencer, and say casually, "I'm late for class."

"I'll walk you." He gives me one of his smiles, the one that makes my stomach go all fluttery, but I see the questions in his eyes. He knows I'm upset.

Good.

"I'll see you later, Charlotte." Tatum walks away quickly, and I know nothing is ever going to be the same between us.

"If I was any other guy, I might be jealous of the way he hangs all over you."

I shrug him off. "Good thing you're not any other guy."

"Hey." He grabs my hand. "What's wrong."

"Um, let's see." I don't want to sound jealous over seeing him with Winslow, or needy by demanding why he hasn't tried to see me again. Instead, I focus on the one thing I have every right to be angry about. "Your douchebag friend paid me a little visit at the coffee shop this morning."

"Prescott?" Spencer winces. "What did he say?"

"That even though you got in my pants on the weekend, you still lost the bet."

"Shit. It's not what you think."

I laugh, but the sound is metallic in my ears as I pull my arm back. "I don't care."

"Prescott is an asshole."

"Yeah. You're right, he is. And he made it clear that I'm not in the same league as you."

"He said that?" Anger tightens his features. "I'll talk to him."

"Whatever." I shake my head and look away, catching Winslow watching us from across the lawn, surrounded by a gaggle of her clones. Each one looks ready to murder me.

Perfect.

"I have to get to class." I sprint toward the old building, not looking back.

But when I sit down in a chair at the back of the lecture hall, I feel a warm body sit next to me. The way my own body reacts, I don't need to look over to know it's Spencer.

"Don't run from me, Charlie."

"Don't follow me, Spencer," I hiss back, ready to get up and move, but the professor comes into the room, and I know if I do I'll make a scene.

"Yeah, there was a bet, but that was before I knew you."

"You think that makes it better?"

A few heads turn around and glare at me.

"Can you leave?" I mumble. "Please."

"Not until you forgive me."

"Fine. I forgive you. Just go."

The professor starts lecturing, and I pull out my notebook and pen.

"You know I have all my lecture notes from this course. I can give them to you."

"I don't want anything from you."

"See. You're still upset."

I exhale heavily. "Being upset means I'd have to care. And I don't."

"Shhh." A girl two rows in from of me shushes before rolling her eyes and turning back to the front.

Spencer leans closer, his breath warm against my ear. "I've missed you."

I grunt, scribbling down what the professor is saying, but I miss half of it because I'm too aware of the way Spencer's leg brushes against mine.

"Come over to my place after your class."

"No."

He chuckles. "You know you're going to say yes eventually. Why fight me?"

I slam my pencil down on my desk and glare at him. "Maybe you should go ask Winslow. You and she looked pretty cozy earlier."

Spencer frowns.

"Is there a problem back there?" the professor asks. "Mr. Beckett, I'm pretty sure you've already taken this course."

"And aced it," Spencer says, giving a cocky grin before sliding out of his seat. "I was just leaving." He leans down and says, "Come over after class and I'll give you more than my notes. I'll give you everything you've been dreaming about since you left my place the other night."

Heat rushes to my face, and I swear some of the people around me heard what he said, because I hear a few sighs, mixed with giggles.

And I'm right back where I started, swooning over a guy who is clearly going to break my heart.

When the lecture is over and I leave the hall, I find Spencer leaning against the wall, waiting for me, and there goes the damn butterflies again, wreaking havoc in my stomach.

He pulls me around a corner, and I'm pressed against the wall, his solid body trapping me before I can even let out a little yelp.

"Spencer——"

His mouth crashes down on mine, hard, fast, his tongue darting across my lips until I open for him.

He groans, "Wasn't lying, Hayes. I missed you."

"This is so wrong."

"Why? Because I make you feel good."

"You make me feel like I'm spinning out of control."

He chuckles against my lips and kisses me again. "Cause you're fighting too hard against me."

He's right. But what are my other options? Give in or run as fast as I can from him. The latter would be the smarter choice, but I already know which way my body and heart are leaning toward.

"Come back to my place."

"I have to study."

"So do I." He kisses my neck.

"If we go to your apartment, I know what you'll want."

He pulls back and frowns. "I'm not pushing you

for sex, Charlie. If I wanted to have you, I would have."

"So you don't want me?"

"You have a way of twisting words." He kisses the tip of my nose. "Yes, Charlie Hayes, I want you. I want to spread that sweet little body of yours out on my bed, eat that delicious pussy again, then fill you so deep and full with my cock that you'll be ruined for all other men. But I'm going to wait until I know you're ready. Does that answer your question?"

I manage to whimper a "yes."

And right now I feel more than ready. I've never wanted a guy like I want Spencer Beckett.

"How about your dorm?" he asks.

I frown up at him. "What?"

"We can go there to study."

"My roommate might be there."

"Your other options are the library or my apartment." He whispers against my ear. "Whatever you choose, there will be some heavy making out going on. So unless you don't mind public displays of affection—"

"Okay, my dorm."

He chuckles and squeezes my ass. "Good girl."

Then he tucks his hand in my back pocket, laying claim to me.

As we walk across campus toward my dorm, the hairs on the back of my neck stand on end and I shiver. Something presses on the back of my skull, a feeling like I'm being watched.

"You cold?" he asks, wrapping an arm over my shoulder.

"Yeah," I mutter, glancing around. For a second I swear I see a hooded figure in the shadows, but when I blink, it's gone. "Let's just get upstairs."

Daphne is out, so the place is ours. I drop my backpack and begin peeling off my layers. Scarf, hat, jacket, sweatshirt.

"Keep it going," Spencer teases playfully as he pulls his slim laptop from his messenger bag.

"Haha. I don't strip for study partners."

Spencer pouts playfully, falling into my bed like he owns it. He reaches under him and pulls out an envelope. "Sorry, I crushed this."

He hands it to me, and I frown. After opening the seal, I pull out a note. All it says is *Glass slippers can crack. Careful Cinderella, yours isn't a happy ending.* "What the heck?"

"What is it?" Spencer asks as I hand him the

warning. He reads it and immediately pulls out his phone. "We need to call campus security."

"Who would write that?"

"I don't know, but someone doesn't like the idea of you spending time with Princeton Charming."

I press a hand to his phone. Maybe Tatum got really weird about the way I ended things at the party and took things to another level. I don't think Tatum would do this … but what if his emotions got the best of him and he did this without thinking. Getting security involved, and finding out it was the star athlete, could cost him more than his reputation.

"I think it was just someone being stupid," I say. "Don't involve campus security, please."

"That's how things get out of control, Charlie. We have to report this."

I exhale. "Please? I'll tell you if anything else weird happens. I promise." Then lifting my eyebrows I say, "What were we saying about stripping?"

He laughs, setting his phone on the bedside table. "We were saying it's way too hot to study fully dressed." He reaches for me, and his hands run under the hem of my shirt. A thrill washes over me as his fingertips brush my skin.

"How do you like to study?" I ask, laughing.

"In my boxer briefs, obviously." His grin is so damn irresistible.

"Fine, but I'm keeping my bra on."

He pulls my shirt off, over my head. "You are so bossy, Charlie Hayes. I like it."

"Why do I get the feeling there won't be much studying taking place today?" I laugh, as his hands run over the lacy cups of my bra.

"Oh there will be studying all right," he says, looking me over. "Me studying every inch of your perfect body."

"You're so cheesy, Spencer Beckett."

"And you're an easy A."

13

SPENCER

AFTER A STUDY SESSION with Charlie that ends with me blue balled harder than I've been since I was fifteen years old, I decide the next time I'm alone with her, I'm not holding back. She wanted to sleep with me instead of reviewing my old lecture notes - but there was no way in hell I was going to take Charlie's virginity on a twin bed in a shared dorm room.

She deserves a hell of a lot more than that. She asked for romance, didn't she?

Still the next week goes by in a blur. She cancels on me once because she has a job interview, and half my weeknights are filled with school commitments. By the time the next Saturday rolls around, I am dying to see her, but I promised my sister we'd Christmas shop.

Me: You can come with. Ava won't mind.

Charlie: Thanks, but I'll pass. Prescott told me about a law office hiring, and I want to get my resume up to par.

My brow creases. Why is he all up in Charlie's business?

Me: Prescott, huh?

Charlie: Yeah, awesome right? He emailed me about it this morning.

Refusing to sound like a jealous ass, I think of a chill response.

Me: Sounds good. How about dinner tonight?

Charlie: Sounds great. Text later?

I haven't exactly had a girlfriend since Winslow, and I'm not saying Charlie is mine, but it feels like we could get there. When we text, it's like we're in a relationship. Like there is mutual trust, respect, courtesy.

And it's really fucking with my mind.

When I pick Ava up from her campus dorm, she can tell something is on my mind.

"You look a million miles away," she says as we drive toward the mall.

"I'm not. I'm right here."

"Yeah? Well good because I need to talk to you."

"Everything okay?" I look over at my little sister, concerned with her tone.

"Not really," she groans. "Mom and Dad found out about my little hospital visit and they are pissed."

"When did this happen?"

"About ten minutes before you picked me up."

"Ah, makes sense why I hadn't heard about it yet."

"Well sorry, but you will. They seem to think I need more *boundaries*." She makes air quotes.

"Which means?"

She scoffs. "They said something about an allowance."

I roll my eyes, turning on my blinker to pull into the crowded mall parking lot. "They think money motivates everyone."

Ava smirks. "Wel,l it motivates you."

Frowning I ask, "What's that supposed to mean?"

"Oh come on, Spence. You always want the fanciest cars, the most expensive clothes, and the most high-end vacations."

Turning off the ignition I look over at my sister. Fendi booties. Gucci bomber jacket. Bottega Veneta handbag. She is wearing twenty grand in clothing, easy.

"Right, I'm the one who is obsessed with money."

Ava rolls her eyes. "Mom buys me this shit. I don't care about it."

We get out of the car, neither of us in a great mood. And as we enter the mall, Christmas music blaring, it doesn't exactly get us in a festive spirit.

"If you don't care about flashy items then why are we at the fanciest shopping center in Jersey?" I ask her.

"Because our mother will hold it against us on Christmas morning if we don't get her something with a label she approves of."

"Fair enough. Then can we just get what we need and get out of here? This mall gives me the creeps. Everyone is so plastic."

Ava twists her lips. "So maybe there is some meat to the rumor about you and your scholarship girl?"

I lift my eyebrows, incredulous. "You know her name. God Ava, she saved your life."

"I know." She smiles, slugging me in the arm as

we wind our way through Bloomingdales. "I was testing you, wanted to see if you'd come to her defense. And you did. You like her."

"Yeah." I clench my jaw. "I don't know what the rumors say, but Charlie deserves more than speculation."

"What does that mean?"

"I don't like the idea of people talking about her behind her back."

We pause at a jewelry counter. "Well, she'll need to get used to it if you plan on spending more time with her. Winslow's claws are out and it's only a matter of time before Mom and Dad get involved."

"Mom and Dad are not getting involved with this," I warn.

"Sure, just like we thought they wouldn't find out about my little trip to the ER. They have eyes and ears everywhere. And they will not be happy about your relationship with Charlotte Hayes. She's a sweetheart, but not at all in your league."

"Ava, you're my sister, but that's too far. You can't put her down, and if our parents come after you for information about her, promise me you'll have my back. Charlie means something to me."

Ava's eyes widen. "Wow, you really like her."

I nod. "Yeah, she's really … special."

Ava gives me a hug. "Of course I have your back, Spencer. You're my big brother." Then she smiles, eyes twinkling. "So what are you getting her for Christmas? Those earrings are gorgeous." Ava points to a pair of solitaire diamonds. "Any girl would die for them."

I smile to myself - yeah right, as if Ava isn't motivated by money.

"No, not Charlie. She'd balk at them."

"So what would she like?" Ava asks. "A Hermes purse? Oh, a cashmere Burberry scarf?"

I shake my head. "We won't find what she'd want here. But I have an idea of where we could go."

Ava's eyes are bright. "Okay, let's finish shopping for Mom, Dad, and Gran and then go get your girl her Christmas gift."

My girl.

It sounds about right.

Later, after the mall shopping is done, Ava and I park in downtown Princeton.

"A record store?" Ava asks as I pull open a door.

"Charlie's a collector."

Ava frowns. "You know Mom and Dad will never approve of her, right?"

I stiffen. "She could win them over."

My sister squeezes my arm. "Oh Spencer, you are so screwed."

Stepping into the record store, I shake my head. I'm falling for Charlie Hayes and my parents are not going to get in the way of that.

14

CHARLIE

DAPHNE STANDS in front of her open wardrobe in her bra and underwear. "I have nothing to wear," she moans.

I roll my eyes, reviewing the open document on my laptop. My resume is as good as it's going to get. There is no way I'm qualified for the job Prescott mentioned. I never interned anywhere impressive and my work experience is the waitress gig and working at my uncle's used car lot back in Michigan. And I wasn't even a salesman. I made coffee runs and took out the trash.

Sure, I have spent tons of hours volunteering over the years - it's in part why I was accepted to Princeton in the first place. I was awarded a Presidential Scholar, but this is a job at a law office and

I'm guessing they want more experience than a glowing transcript.

"Charlotte, are you even listening?"

"What?" I ask, focusing on my half naked roommate.

"What should I wear tonight?"

"Where are you going?"

She groans. "You are so out of it. What has you so distracted?"

I close my laptop and sit up. "I still haven't found a job."

She frowns. "I can give you money."

"I don't want your money." And I don't. It's not that I'm above help, but Daphne's handouts have strings. She doesn't even want the money back, the currency she is most interested in is time.

"Well if you change your mind." She grabs a skin-tight black knit dress and pulls it over her head. "You should come out with me tonight. I miss you. And you'd love Kai and Caleb."

"The crew guys?"

"Yeah. And they are so yummy." She wiggles her brows at me. "And there's plenty to share."

I can't help but laugh. She's shameless.

"I think I'm going to meet up with Spencer."

Daphne sits next to me on the bed. "Really, I thought you were over him?"

"I thought so too, but then we met up last week to study and…"

"You share the same class? I thought he was a grad student."

"He is, he was just helping." I feel heat rise to my cheeks, remembering our study session… we spent more time exploring one another's bodies then we did reviewing any notes.

"You like him?" she asks.

I shrug. "I mean… yeah? Honestly, I think if it comes up … I'll sleep with him."

"Wait, what!" Daphne's jaw drops. "You'll part with your V-card if Princeton Charming wants it?"

"It's not just about what *he* wants. God, Daph. I want it to. I mean, he's *really* hot."

"And arrogant. And cocky. And way too conceited. You need someone wholesome, someone with morals and—"

"Hey! You don't get to judge. You're going to have a threesome with two jocks tonight."

"Yeah, but I'm not Charlotte Hayes. Home-grown sweetheart with more class than half the girls at Princeton. You're too good for Spencer Beckett."

"Seems like everyone thinks the opposite."

Daphne purses her lips at me and takes my hand. "You really don't see it, do you?"

"What?"

"You." The way she looks at me makes me feel uneasy, but I'm not sure why. "You're just—"

There's a knock at the door and it gives me the perfect excuse to pull my hand away and stand.

Tatum is pacing in the hallway when I open the door.

"Hey." I frown up at him, remembering the cryptic note I found under my pillow. I haven't seen him since, and the way he fidgets nervously now, my suspicions that he's the one who left it are strengthened.

"Hey." He rubs the back of his neck. "Look, I feel like I owe you an apology."

"For what?"

"I've been..." He winces. "I guess I've been jealous since you started hanging out with Beckett."

"Just cause I'm seeing him, doesn't mean we can't be friends."

"So you are dating him?"

"I don't know. But I like him."

"The guy is a player, Charlie. He'll hurt you."

"Maybe, but that's my choice."

He shakes his head. "Charlie—"

"Tatum, I'm a big girl. I appreciate you worrying about me. But, it's not necessary."

He grunts. "Just don't say I didn't warn you when you come crying to me. It won't end well."

His words are similar to what the note said. *Careful Cinderella, yours isn't a happy ending.*

"Did you..." I chew on the inside of my lip before asking, "Did you leave me a note?"

He frowns. "What kind of a note?"

"In my room. I found...never mind."

"I haven't been in your room, Charlie." He grins then, his playfulness returning. "And I wouldn't say no if you asked me."

I laugh. "Not happening, Tatum."

"A guy can dream." He winks before turning and starting down the hall, but stops and says over his shoulder, "Oh, I almost forgot to tell you. The dorm is having a Secret Santa again, and I entered your name."

A groan slips passed my lips. "Thanks," I mutter sarcastically.

But it reminds me that I still haven't figured out how I'm going to afford to get home for the holidays. I really hope that this job Prescott mentioned pans out. After his little stunt in the coffee shop, I was surprised to get his message. But since then he's been unusually nice, which I assume is because Spencer had a talk with him.

When I walk back into my room, Daphne is holding my phone. She jumps slightly, eyes widening when she sees me before holding it out to me.

"Sorry, I thought it was mine. Spencer just texted."

"Thanks," I mutter, taking my phone from her and reading Spencer's text.

He's just finishing a class and wants to meet me in front of Rockefeller College. I grab my jacket and say a quick goodbye to Daphne, who looks totally put out that I'm meeting up with Spencer.

Sometimes I swear the girl is more high maintenance than having a boyfriend. Not that I have experience to compare it, but I can't imagine any guy being as clingy as Daphne is.

It's dark out when I leave the dorm and snowflakes dance in the wind. Dry leaves crunch under my boots as I head toward the old building. The campus is relatively quiet, and I smile at a group of three girls who walk past me before turning down the pathway that's usually lit up at this time of night.

But two of the street light bulbs are burnt out

and I swear I see something move in the shadows.

I think about turning around, going another way, but it would take me an extra ten minutes and my fingers and cheeks are already numb with cold.

Swallowing hard and hurrying down the sidewalk, I let out a small laugh when I make it to a well-lit area.

"Since when is Charlie Hayes afraid of shadows?" I mumble to myself. But I have this weird feeling at the base of my skull, like the one I felt a few days ago, as if someone is following me.

Footsteps fall behind me. Crunch. Crunch. Crunch. In time with my own.

I glance over my shoulder, and this time I know I'm not imagining it when a figure steps back into the shadows.

My throat constricts, and I start running. Maybe I'm overreacting, but I'd rather be safe than sorry. But when I glance back again, I miss the curb in front of me, and I sprawl onto the pavement.

"Jesus, Hayes. You okay?" Large hands help me up, and adrenaline and fear has me pushing the person away. "Whoa," Prescott says, frowning down at me. "Who are you running from?"

I glance behind me, but there's no one there. "I..." Shaking my head, I try to take a step back from Spencer's friend, but he doesn't let me go. "Where did you come from?"

His brows form a deep V. "Class. Why?"

"I thought..." God, maybe I'm losing my mind. But first the note, and now this.

"You're trembling."

"I'm fine." I glance down at where his fingers curl around my upper arm. "You can let go of me now."

He releases me and puts his hands up, giving me an arrogant grin. "Just trying to help."

"Thanks."

"Heard you applied for that job."

"Yeah. I appreciate you letting me know about it."

"I can think of a way you can make it up to me."

"Excuse me?"

"It's a joke, Hayes. But if Spencer isn't man enough to take that V-card of yours, I'm more than willing to do the job."

"You're lucky she doesn't have a tray of champagne," some guy I've seen hanging around Spencer and Prescott says behind me, chuckling. "You'd totally be wearing it now."

"You're both lucky I don't have a can of mace

on me."

Prescott laughs. "You're feisty. No wonder Spencer likes you. I'm serious Hayes, once he dumps your ass to the curb, give me a call. He might have the whole charming bit down, but I'm a much better lay."

The guy whose name I don't know, smacks Prescott's back. "That's not what your sister said."

"Fuck you."

"No thanks. I prefer blondes with big tits..."

I turn on my heels, not able to listen to another second of their banter. But I do hear the guy say to Prescott as I'm walking away, "Since when doesn't Beckett share?"

But it's Prescott's comment that sends chills down my spine. "He will. I just have to be patient with this one."

Their laughter echoes behind me, and I find myself almost sprinting, barely looking where I'm going, because anger has me seeing red.

An arm wraps around my waist and I let out a little shriek when I'm pulled back against a muscular chest.

"Let go," I yell, spinning around and ready to knee my attacker in the balls.

"It's me." Concerned blue eyes blink down at

me, and I can't help but collapse against Spencer's chest, and let out a shaky breath. "What the hell happened?" He places his hand under my chin and lifts my face up toward his. "Are you okay?"

"I'm fine. I just...I thought someone was following me. Then I tripped and fell. Then Prescott—"

"What did he do?"

"Nothing. He just...was Prescott."

He holds my face, studying me. "You're sure you're all right?"

I chew on my bottom lip and nod.

"Okay." He presses his lips to my forehead, then pulls back. "I thought we could go out for dinner."

"Actually..." I hesitate, wanting to be alone with Spencer, but also knowing what will happen if I suggest it. "I was thinking we could go back to your place."

He frowns slightly. "You sure?"

I know what he's asking.

"Yeah. I am."

He kisses me. Soft. Gentle. And I swear there's emotion in it. Maybe I'm just fooling myself, thinking I'm any different than all the other girls he's been with. But the way he looks at me, I feel...special.

But then Prescott's words roll through my head.

"Did you tell Prescott I'm a virgin?" I ask.

"No. Why?" Anger flares in his eyes. "Did he say something to you?"

He'd thought at the coffee shop that I'd had sex with Spencer. So, what changed?

"It's fine."

"It's not fine if he upset you."

I shiver. "You and him, do you usually...share girls."

"Going to kill that asshole. Is that what he said to you?"

"Is it true?"

Spencer sighs. "Yeah. We have."

My insides flip flop. Is that what he expects of me? I know it's not uncommon. I may be a virgin, but I've read books, and I've heard stories. I mean Daphne is my roommate, she's the queen of orgies. But that's not me.

"I...I can't do that." The thought of Prescott's hands on me sends a chill down my back.

"I'd never expect that from you." Spencer is still cupping my jaw. "Ever. You understand me, Charlie? I don't want anyone ever touching you, but me."

There's a possessiveness in his words that makes my heart race.

He rests his forehead against mine and closes his eyes. I can feel the tension rolling off him. Finally, he says, "I'll drive you back to your dorm."

"No." I shake my head. "I still want to go back to your place."

"You sure?"

"Yes. But I'm starving. So I hope you have more than just beer in your fridge."

He smirks. "Only you would call Sapporo's Space Barley, *just beer*."

"And only Princeton Charming would have beer in his fridge that was made in space."

"Only the barley was grown in space."

I shake my head at him. "You know you're ridiculous, right?"

"It's all part of my charm." He winks at me, then takes my hand as we walk toward where he parked his Mercedes. A car that probably cost him as much as my parents' house.

I'll never fit into his world.

But as he wraps an arm around me and pulls me close, I can't help but feel that it doesn't matter, because I fit with him.

Oh, you are so going to have your heart broken, Charlie Hayes, my brain warns.

I know it's inevitable. But I'm already falling.

The note that was left under my pillow wasn't just a warning, it's the unavoidable reality. There's no happily ever after with Spencer Beckett. But then when is there ever? This isn't a fairy tale, and I'm no Cinderella. But that doesn't mean I can't have a little fun with the Prince before he gallops off into the sunset with his real princess.

I chuckle to myself as I fasten my seatbelt.

"What's so funny?" Spencer asks, cocking a brow as he starts the keyless ignition.

"I think some of your corniness is rubbing off on me."

He grins. "Is that so?"

"Yeah."

"I've got something else I wouldn't mind rubbing off on you." He winks before pressing his foot to the pedal and speeding toward his apartment.

Exaggeratedly, I groan, but I can't help the smile that tugs at my lips. "Like I said, corny."

"Yeah, but you love me for it."

He has no idea how close to the truth he is.

15

SPENCER

ON THE WAY back to my place we stop at a grocery store. "We're going to need sustenance," I tell her.

She chuckles, but as we wind through Whole Foods her fingers find mine, and a current of desire spreads through me. God, there is something about this girl that has me dizzy. We pick out wine and cheeses, crackers and salami. I've never done something so simple with a girl - buy groceries with plans to spend a night together at my place. I'm one-night stands and hook-ups. Charlie makes me want to slow down time, to draw this out. To savor every last second.

"And we need dessert," she says, pausing at the bakery. Cakes and pies and tarts in the display case. "What's your poison?"

"I have a sweet tooth, but Charlie, I think you'll be enough sugar for me tonight."

She laughs, stepping closer, on her tiptoes, ruffling my hair with her hand. "Sorry, Spence. I need more than that. I'm thinking cupcakes. Extra frosting. Sprinkles."

I smile, loving that she tells me what she wants. She isn't coy, playing a part - she is Charlotte Hayes, through and through. "I guess we are gonna be burning a lot of calories."

Her head falls back, her easy laughter filling the grocery store, and I kiss her. Unable to resist. Her mouth is warm and wanting and I feel my cock grow hard as my hands hold her waist, wanting to take control of this moment. This night.

"We need to get out of here," I groan in her ear. When I look in her eyes, I see they have grown heavy with need. She nods, licking those full lips of hers and she grabs a package of gourmet cupcakes. In seconds we're at the checkout and I can't keep my hands and eyes off of her. My palm is on the small of her back, my mouth on her neck. I don't give a fuck about public displays of affection. Charlie is here for me and I'm here for her. Tonight is only about us.

In the parking lot, paper bags in hand for our

at-home picnic, I squeeze her ass as we walk to my car. She giggles with excitement, but as a familiar Tesla pulls into the parking lot, I groan.

"Let's get out of here, Charlie," I say, ushering her to my Mercedes.

But Winslow pulls in to the spot next to mine.

As I open Charlie's door, Winslow steps out of her car. "Are you fucking kidding me, Spencer?" Her words are haughty and heated, my eyes move between hers and Charlie's.

"Can we not do this?" I plead with the girl I spent every summer of my life with. The girl I lost my virginity to. The girl who held my hand when my brother died.

Dammit, we have history, but I don't want it to repeat. Not anymore.

"I've heard the rumors, but God, you're really going to do this to your poor parents?"

I take a harder look at Winslow. Her hair's in a messy bun, she's in Uggs and leggings and under the lamplight overhead, I can tell she's not wearing any makeup. Honestly, she looks better than I've seen her in a long time - but it's so out of character I know something is wrong.

"Spencer?" Charlie's voice brings me back to the moment.

I nod, knowing where my allegiance lies tonight. "Take care, Winnie," I say, refusing to give her any more of my time. As I get into my leather seat, I look over at Charlie. "Sorry about that," I tell her.

"It's okay. I'm not scared of Winslow."

My lips twitch. "No? You might be the only person I know who isn't."

She shakes her head. "The chip on my shoulder has made me tough, Spencer Beckett. I'm not scared of a little friendly competition."

I cup her cheek and kiss her softly. "There is no competition tonight, Charlie. Tonight, it's only about me and you."

———

ONCE IN THE HOUSE, the food is left on the counter, forgotten. The moment we are alone, without any exes or grocery store clerks to get in our way, we can't hold back. I want to fuck this little virgin nice and slow. All night long. Over and over again. We may not be in a rush, but we are ready to get there.

"My room," I tell her. "That's where you belong right now."

She nods obediently like she wants the direction. Oh, I'll tell her what to do. We move up the stairs, my cock growing with need as I watch her little ass take each step.

In my room, I undress her slowly.

"You're killing me, Spencer," she laughs as I pull her sweater up over her head, as I ease down her jeans, her panties. As I unclasp her bra. My virgin is naked before me and my jaw clenches, taking in the sight of her.

"Goddammit you're perfect," I tell her, my hands running over her bare skin. I undress quickly and she clucks her tongue.

"So you take your time with me and don't give me the same pleasure?"

I shake my head. "I promise to give you plenty of pleasure tonight, sweetheart."

Guiding her hand, she wraps her fingers around my shaft and her eyelids flutter. "You're really…"

"Big? Thick? Hard? All of those adjective work just fine," I tease, kissing her earlobe.

"I was going to say huge." She laughs, her eyes sparkling and I laugh too and I have never, ever been like this with a woman before. Had so much flirty fun. So much ease, even in a moment of passion.

Charlie is effortless and comforting and even

though this is her first time, it's like she isn't scared. She isn't hesitating or anxious. And she is ready. The pride that fills my chest is unprecedented. She feels safe with me and that makes me want to be worthy of her. To be the man she needs.

I fist her hair, lifting it up so I can leave kisses along her neck, and we move toward the bed, my hand between her legs, feeling her wetness, her need. "I've been getting off to the memory of your sweet pussy for days, Charlotte Hayes," I confess.

Her breathing slows as I move over her petite frame, I press a finger against her needy entrance. "I've been so tense," she murmurs. "For the last week, my dreams have been my never-ending sexually repressed fantasy. Every night."

"You've been dreaming about me?"

She nods, her tits rising as I run my fingers up and down her tight folds. "Mmhhmm," she answers and a grin spreads across my face. "You're easily swayed with compliments, aren't you?"

"I'm like everyone else. I like to be thought of."

"I wasn't thinking of you," she moans as I finger her warmth. Her clit is so sweet and tender and her back arches as I tease the nub mercilessly. "I was fantasizing," she tells me. "About this. Our first time. I wanted it to be you."

My cock aches at her words, and I want her like I've never wanted another woman. With a desperation that unnerves me.

"Charlie," I growl as I sheath myself, I press my mouth to her slick pussy. Kissing her before I fill her up. If only she understood how I feel right now. More than a prince, with her beneath me, giving herself to me, I feel like a goddamn king.

When I move my cock inside her, slowly as to not hurt my virgin girl, I look into her eyes.

What I see terrifies me as much as it ignites me. When I look into Charlie's eyes, I see the possibility for a forever that I've never imagined for myself.

Goddammit, I'm falling for her. Hard.

And I don't care if I'm going to crash.

Right now, this falling feels so damn good.

16

CHARLIE

He moves inside of me, slowly, making my body ignite with need as he deepens his hold on me. On my heart. I know he's a man with a reputation that should scare me, but under him, against him, filled with him, I feel secure.

And I also feel like every single inch of my skin has been consumed with a fire I didn't realize was possible. My body opens to him, and my heart pounds with excitement as he rocks against me, as his mouth plants kisses along my neck and my breasts, sending a crazy rush of pleasure through my veins.

"You're so tight," he growls as he moves deeper inside me, his thick cock filling me so entirely that my body can't help but whimper with relief. It's like for the first time ever my body is being given exactly what it wants. Spencer Beckett, in his entirety.

"Oh, Spence, oh, ohhhh," I cry as he laces his fingers with mine, pinning my hand over my head. Eyes locked, heart beating hard, bodies pulsing. This is the moment I waited so long for.

And God, I'm glad I held out.

Spencer takes control of my body, giving me what I need, and I don't have to ask. He wraps my legs around him, his palm on my ass, he takes me soft, then hard, in a rhythm of his own making. A rhythm that unravels me until I am jelly in his hands. Until my pussy is begging for release. Until he gives me exactly what I want. An orgasm washes over me and my toes curl and his thick hard cock pulses deeper inside me taking me where I want to go.

Over the edge, with him.

Again and again.

We make love and it isn't painful, it is pleasure personified - Spencer Beckett has a reputation for a reason. He knows how to fuck and make a woman come.

He knows how to make me scream his name.

"Oh Spence, yes," I cry as we finish together, his

cock thrumming inside me and he cradles me in his arms as he comes to the same edge I'm on.

"Goddammit, Charlie," he moans, kissing me hard. He rolls to the side of me, both of us working to catch our breath. "What the hell was that?"

I roll over as he removes the condom. "What do you mean?"

He shakes his head, pulling me to him. "That wasn't just sex. That was a goddamn light show. Fucking fireworks."

Heat rises to my cheeks, and I bite my lower lip, a smile spreading across my face. "So cheesy, Spence."

He nods. "Yeah, but so true." He kisses the tip of my nose and that right there gets me wet all over again. He isn't what I expected. And if these moves of his are a part of his quintessential charm, I get the appeal. But when he looks at me, when he takes my hand and pulls me from his bed, wrapping me in a robe and leading me to the kitchen, I can't help but feel like what we just shared was special for him too.

He's naked as he opens the wine and feeds me grapes, and the grin on my face only widens.

These aren't canned moves.

Are they?

I don't want to believe they are. Because when he picks me up from the floor and sets me on his kitchen counter, kissing me again like it's the first time our lips have ever collided, sending sparks over my skin, sending a flash of want over me all over again, I can't imagine this is all an act.

It feels like the beginning of a love story. *My love story.*

"Why are you smiling so hard?" he asks.

"I'm just...happy," I admit.

Spencer grins as he starts to slice the cheese and salami. He hands me a cracker with slices of both. "Eat," he tells me with a wink. "Sustenance."

I do as he says, eager for more of his attention.

Being with him is unexpectedly easy. Sure, the wine that I take a sip of cost more than I made in a night working as a waitress, but despite being from completely different worlds, we seem to...fit.

Or maybe I just want to believe that. Holding onto the fairy tale for at least tonight.

Spencer moves closer, undoes the tie on my robe, the terry cloth falling from my shoulder. He plants kisses on my collarbone as the robe is discarded, and plucks my nipple, sending excitement to my core.

I love the feeling of his hard body pressed

against me. I drag my fingers down his chest, over his abs, sucking my bottom lip between my teeth when I notice that he's already hard again.

"You are so naked," I tell him. Every inch of him is chiseled, perfect. Tanned and toned and just looking at him makes my pussy tingle with excitement. His cock is so thick, so big - and I know that I'm always calling him cheesy and that calling his shaft big and thick is as cheesy as it gets - but it is.

Princeton Charming has a sword and he certainly knows how to use it.

He smirks. "You know it's not polite to stare."

I close my eyes, blushing. Still, all I want to do with Spencer is flirt and fuck. Crass maybe, but it's the honest truth.

"I must have forgotten all my manners," I tell him, then tease, "I'm so sorry. How ever can I make it up to you?"

"You don't need to apologize, Princess," he says, stroking himself. "But if you want a better look, all you need to do is ask."

I twist my lips, loving his games. "I see. Then, can you please help me get closer?"

He growls with desire, and lifts me from the counter, taking me to the carpeted floor of the living room. I love how in control he is. "Your wish is my command."

Naked, on my knees, I take his cock in my hand, wanting his warm cum to slide down my throat, wanting to pleasure him the way he has pleasured me. My pussy sings with anticipation as I open my mouth and take him.

He rests his hands on my head, and I begin to suck him in the way I dreamt about doing all week. My mouth is full of him and my pussy begins to drip as I suck him the way I sense he needs. I take him in fully, and the head of his cock hits the back of my throat. I moan with delight as he groans above me. His shaft is hard and veiny, velvety smooth and rigid at the same time.

I feel so beautiful as I look up at him, my mouth full of his cock, our eyes meeting, salty precum hits my tongue and it makes me suck harder, wanting more. More. More. Wanting to make him remember me forever, wanting to get him off until he can't think straight, until his mind is only filled with thoughts of me.

My want for him in this moment is overwhelming, all-encompassing and it makes me dizzy. My singular motivation: being his.

He loves it, I can tell, because as he reaches his

climax, he thrusts deep against my mouth, calling my name as he comes. "Fuck me, Charlie," he begs, and I do. My mouth fills with his salty release and I swallow him, my belly already needing more.

He pulls out, and I lick my lips, my body hot and pulsing. I press a finger to my pussy, needing the relief, the same way as him. He sees me touching myself and his cock twitches.

I smile, my clit aching. "I thought you said it was rude to stare?"

He laughs, moving to the floor. "Give me that pussy, Princess."

When I remove my finger, he takes my hand and sucks it, groaning with want as he does and a thrill rushes over me. He likes this just as much as I do.

"Come here," he tells me as we lie down on the floor. "No," he says, rolling me on top of him. "Fuck me like this." He moves me so I straddle him, and he grabs a condom from a side table, rolling it on.

"Prepared, are we?"

He laughs. "Always."

"Good," I whisper as he lifts my hips, he guides me down. This is different, sitting down on him. I gasp, the pleasure so different, so intense. So damn good.

"Oh God, Spencer," I whimper as he smiles up at me.

"Good right?"

His thumb presses to my clit as I begin to swivel my hips ever so slowly. The sensation so all-encompassing I forget myself. My fingers run through my hair and I ride him, coming hard as I move.

"You're so fucking wet, girl," he groans, smacking my ass as I come for him. He plays with my breasts, drawing me lower so he can suck them. The pleasure is so intense as he sucks my hard nipples, I grind against his massive cock.

"You feel so good," I cry as he rolls me to my back, pinning my hands over my head. His body is perfection and somehow we fit together. There are a million reasons him and I won't work in the real world, but tonight, the real world is miles away. Tonight, it's just Spencer and me. It's what we both need, what we want. It's about more than sex - it's an escape.

"You're so beautiful," he tells me as our bodies reach an entirely new rhythm. Faster. Harder. Deeper. More.

I pant as I come, dripping for him like I didn't

know was possible, and when he thrusts inside me, the pleasure rolls over us both, the release so intense, so deep and real that we collapse after. Satiated, full, and so utterly happy.

I'm falling for Spencer Beckett, and I have an inkling the feeling is mutual.

17

SPENCER

CHARLIE IS FAST ASLEEP, cheek resting on my chest, her breathing low, and her lips twitch up slightly before she murmurs something incoherent. I run my thumb over her cheek and sigh. So damn beautiful.

I want to join her in her dreams, but as hard as I try to sleep, I can't. My mind is racing, and my heart feels like it's being squeezed in my chest.

Who the hell is this girl? And what has she done to me?

I didn't doubt the sex would be good. Knew the second I saw her at the gala that she was fire. More than that, she's sunlight and goodness and everything that I didn't know I needed, but now never want to live without.

And then I'd kissed her.

Hell, I knew in that second she would undo me.

Because Princeton Charming doesn't kiss.

Or date.

And I liked my life.

Bullshit, Beckett, you've been walking around numb since Ethan died, a voice in my head says.

But with Charlie, I feel again. And it's some scary shit. Allowing another person control of your heart.

My phone buzzes on the dresser, making Charlie stir.

I frown and glance at the clock. It's late. But I always try and answer my calls, just in case it's Ava needing something.

The number displayed on the screen isn't one I recognize, but I do know the area code - France. Shit, that's where my parents are, on some business meeting with the current minister of Culture. I'm sure my mother is eating that shit up.

"Hi Mom," I say, answering the call as I walk out of the bedroom and shutting the door behind me.

She doesn't waste any time chewing into me. "Why didn't you call me when Ava was in the hospital?"

"Because she was fine," I sigh, grabbing a water bottle from the fridge and uncapping it.

"She had alcohol poisoning. How could you let that happen?"

"Ava's nineteen. It's not like I can follow her around campus monitoring her every move."

"Do you have any idea how bad it'll look on your father if the press found out?"

That's what she's really worried about, not that her underage daughter drank to the point where she was puking her guts out.

"And you," my mom continues, sounding like she's about to cry, which is something else she's mastered over the years. The art of manipulation is another Beckett trait. "What are you thinking, hanging around that...that waitress?"

I grind my back teeth. "I'm not sure what Ava told you—"

"Ava didn't tell me. Winslow called, said you were making a fool of yourself over this girl. Flaunting her in public."

I should have known Winslow would call her.

"Mom, it's late. Can we do this in the morning?"

"You're just like your father was. Needing to sow your wild oats—"

"Mom." I move into the living room and sit down on the couch. "I'm not having this conversation with you."

"I understand the need. But you're twenty-three, Spencer, it's time you start thinking about settling down. Winslow——"

"Winslow and I are over. We have been for years."

"She loves you."

No, she was really in love with Ethan. But I don't tell my mom that. Or that I found the two of them together a few months before he died. She'd always wanted him. I knew it. Saw it. And honestly, other than a bruised ego, I hadn't cared. That she's suddenly taken a new interest in me sends up a dozen red flags.

Sure, I'll always care about her, as a friend, but that's it.

"Winslow loves the idea of me, Mom. She'd be just as happy on the arm of any other senator's son's arm."

My mother clucks her tongue. "One day you'll be running for office, and you'll need someone like Winslow beside you."

Except I don't want to run for office. I fucking hate politics. But I'm pretty sure my parents will disown me if I ever admit it to them. And honestly, I have no clue what else to do with my life.

"You're a Beckett. You have a duty to make this world a better place. But you have to play by the rules. Haven't I taught you that?"

"Yeah, Mom. I know your rules."

She sighs. "You have so much potential, my sweet boy. I want you to be happy."

The words sound good, almost like she cares. But I know the truth. It's not my happiness she wants, it's my obedience. To join the long list of Beckett politicians who *made a difference*.

And shit, I want to make a difference in this messed up world. Just not in the way my parents want me to. Fancy parties, rubbing elbows with assholes who only care about getting their bills passed for their own agenda. Putting on fake smiles, campaigning for issues I don't believe in, in order to gain the popular vote. It's all bullshit.

Yeah, I know how to play the game, but I don't want to anymore.

But guilt, responsibility and the constant need of my parents' approval have always superseded my own wants. Not to mention that they still control my bank account.

"Your father and I will be home next week," my

mom is still going on, but I've drowned out most of what she's said. "We're having a small gathering on Saturday. I expect both you and Ava to be there."

An icy numbness has crept into my chest, the way it always does whenever I get one of my mother's calls. But it's better than the sense of complete and bitter disappointment from my father. Thank God, he only calls when my mother feels like I'm not living up to the Beckett name.

So I pretend.

Always fucking pretending.

"Yeah, sure," I mutter, wanting to end this call. Needing to get back to Charlie. Wrap my arms around the girl, and feel something more than the constant battering of expectations that surround me and my family.

Because that's one thing the Becketts are good at - *secrets, lies, manipulation, and expectations.*

I used to think it was because of the political face my family has to present, but I'm starting to wonder if it isn't something that's ingrained into our DNA. The joke of it all is that we're all playing the game, but no one's rules are the same.

Win at any cost. Even if it means being miserable.

After I've hung up, I walk back to the bedroom

and lean against the doorframe, watching Charlie sleep.

Sweet.

Innocent.

Perfect.

She was right when she said she didn't belong in my world. She's too damn good for it. Too damn good for me.

But I'm a selfish bastard, always wanting what I shouldn't have. Taking without thinking about the consequence.

That's how you survive in my world. Taking. Scheming. Conniving.

Winslow's call to my mom was a warning. I know it. Just the start of what she'll do to get what she thinks she wants - me.

Something stirs inside me. A primal need to protect Charlie. From Winslow, from my parents, even from me.

I text Winslow.

Me: I know you called my mom. Stay the fuck out of my business. Or you and I are done.

Only a few seconds pass before the ellipses start bouncing, then a message pops up.

Winnie: I'm trying to protect you. You

can screw whoever you like, Spencer, but flaunting her in public...think about what people will say. You're Spencer Beckett and she's a nobody.

Me: Last warning, Win.

The ellipses bounce, then stop, and a few minutes go by before another text pops up.

Winnie: It's not just you you're hurting. Think about how this looks on me.

I don't respond, even though my fingers are itching to text back. In a fucked up way, she's right. It's always been Winslow who I've called whenever I needed a date. Sure, we both usually ended up in someone else's bed at the end of the night. But as far as society believes, we're together, the perfect couple. Primed and polished for a life in politics.

Another goddamn lie. One that I need to set straight. But I know the second I do, the blood-hounds will be all over Charlie. The girl is tough, but she has no idea how merciless my world truly is.

I scrub a palm over my face then back through my hair. If I was a better man, I'd end things between us now.

"Spencer?" Charlie stirs in bed, rubbing her eyes. "What's wrong?"

"Nothing," I say, crawling back into bed beside her, and pulling her into my arms.

She snuggles against me, her body fitting mine perfectly.

I never let girls sleep here. But if I had my way, I'd never let Charlie leave my bed. Because when she's with me, everything seems right. I just pray to God that my need for her isn't the thing that'll destroy her.

18

CHARLIE

"OUCH." I wake up to Spencer nipping my shoulder.

"Time to wake up, sleepy head." He smacks my ass playfully as he rolls out of bed and struts around the bedroom toward his walk-in closet.

"You kicking me out already?" I tease, but a sliver of insecurity races through me.

He comes out of the closet wearing a pair of low riding sweatpants. "You got a test tomorrow in Davidson's class, right?"

"Yeah." I sit up. "Crap. I almost forgot about that. I should be studying—"

"Not until we have breakfast." He crawls across the bed, trapping me from being able to dart and find my clothes, which are still scattered around his room. "Then I can help you. I took that class two years ago."

"If I stay, I doubt there will be much studying done. And I can't let my grades slip."

He kisses me and I can't help the moan that rumbles from my throat. Spencer chuckles. "Ninety percent studying, ten percent sex. Scout's honor."

"I have a hard time believing you were ever a scout."

He rolls on his back taking me with him so that I'm straddling his hips, and I can feel his erection against my pussy through the cotton of his pants.

"And this is why me staying is a bad idea."

His hands roam over my body, cupping my breasts, and I'm already wet for him, needing him inside me. But I'm also sore from last night, and I was telling him the truth, I can't let my grades slip. I'm already struggling in Davidson's class. I need a good grade on this test.

"I don't even have my books here."

"Like I said, I have the notes. And I'm not ready to give you up just yet."

Just yet? His words imply that it's coming. His ultimate rejection. And I'm not ready for that either.

"Okay. But I need breakfast. And coffee. Oh, and clothes would help too."

He grins up at me. "I prefer you like this."

"And I prefer not failing Theories of Global Justice."

"I won't let that happen. I got a ninety-two in that class."

"Seriously?"

He chuckles as he rolls me over, then gets out of bed, returning to his closet. When he comes back, he's holding a t-shirt that says Property of Princeton. He hands it to me and winks. "Just in case you forget who you belong to."

I raise an eyebrow and try not to show how his words make butterflies take flight in my stomach. "You laying claim?"

He just chuckles, pulling me to him, and before I get the shirt over my head, I am in his arms, once again and his mouth is on mine.

His kisses remind me that the last thing I want to do is leave this townhouse. As he runs his hands over my bare back, I think that ninety percent studying, ten percent sex sounds just about right.

I SPEND the day on Spencer's couch, legs draped over his lap as he helps me study. I'm actually shocked at how smart he is. Figured the infamous Princeton Charming was only here because his parents could afford to bribe the dean of admittance.

"You really know this stuff," I say.

"I'm not just good looks and charm, sweetheart." He taps his temple. "Eight years of the top boarding schools in the country have to account for something."

"Schools?"

He shrugs. "I may have gotten kicked out of a couple."

"For what?"

"I wasn't always as well behaved as I am now."

I chuckle. "You're still trouble."

He pulls me onto his lap and nuzzles his nose against the side of my neck. "What makes you say that?"

"I've heard the rumors." I wrap my arms around his neck and shift so that I'm straddling him.

"You shouldn't believe everything you hear."

I can feel his cock twitch under me. "So you

weren't the one who duct taped the academic dean's car during frosh week?"

He smirks. "Prescott may have had a hand in that one."

"Was it you who turned the Fountain of Freedom into a ball pit?"

"Okay, that was me."

I laugh. "And let's not forget all the girls you've—"

He slaps my ass, hard. "I'd rather not bring up other chicks when I'm with you."

"I'm not the jealous type, Spencer. I knew when I started this with you that you weren't exactly...innocent."

His lips thin as he looks up at me. "No, Charlie. I'm anything but innocent."

"You may be the first guy I...well, you know. But I've kissed other people, too."

"Kissing isn't exactly what I was talking about. And I don't want to think about you with other guys, either."

"Jealous?" I tease.

He frowns. "Yeah."

"Really? Why, it's just kissing, it's not like—"

"Kissing is more intimate than sex, Charlie."

"Um, I don't think so."

He sighs and cups the back of my head drawing my face closer to his. "Sex is just...fucking. But kissing..." He brushes his lips against mine. "It means something."

Despite the way my insides flip flop, I tease, "Well, I'm sure you've kissed your share of girls."

"No."

"No?"

He shrugs. "You're only the second girl I've kissed."

"Oh." It's hard for me to wrap my head around his confession. And even though I know I shouldn't ask, know that I really don't want to know, I ask, "Who was the first?"

His lips purse and he hesitates before answering. "Winslow."

I chew on my bottom lip. "So you two were serious?"

He shrugs. "She wanted to be."

"And you?"

"She'll always mean something to me, but I didn't love her the way she wanted. The way she deserves."

So much for saying I'm not the jealous type. The green monster wriggles in my stomach and tightens my throat.

"Your families, they're close, right?" I can't help but ask.

Spencer groans. "Something like that. Our families have this idea in their head that I'm gonna be some state senator. Winslow is a part of their mastermind plot. Power couple, taking over DC."

My lips twitch as I take in his explanation. It's not exactly giving me confidence in this lasting longer than a fling. Which I knew when I came over here. Still, when Spencer held me in his arms last night, I really could see us as more than a hook-up.

He's only kissed two people.

Sure, Winslow is one of them.

But the other one is me.

That has to mean something, doesn't it?

"Look, the point is that I don't want that life," he says, his fingers laced with mine. "I have a different ambition."

"You don't want to be a politician?"

"I don't know." He shrugs. "You'll think it's dumb." When he leans back on the couch, his cheeks redden slightly, and he looks away.

"Wait, are you embarrassed?"

"I've just never talked about it with anyone."

"Okay, now you have to tell me."

He groans. "Fine, but don't laugh."

"Promise," I say, crossing my heart with my finger.

"I want to help people. And not the kind of help politicians give. I want to be on the ground floor. Really helping. I'd love to have a non-profit where people in crisis could get the services they need. Everything I'm learning right now in poli-sci points to inequality between the rich and poor and..." He trails off, running a hand over his jaw. "I don't know. I'm not qualified, I know that. But..."

I can't help but smile, his confession confirms that there is more than meets the eye when it comes to Spencer Beckett. I straddle him, wanting to look in his eyes. "The arrogant prince has a soft side, I wouldn't have guessed."

He exhales. "Well don't go telling anyone. I have a reputation, you know."

"I know." I run my fingers through his hair. "I won't tell a soul that you're secretly a bleeding-heart. Can you imagine what would happen if that got out?" I gasp exaggeratedly as Spencer begins to tickle me, sending us both into a fit of laughter.

"You are trouble, Charlie Hayes. Trouble."

We fall to the floor, cracking up as Spencer's phone buzzes. He reaches for it and looks at the text. Groaning, he locks it and sets it aside.

"What's up?" I ask.

"Nothing, just Prescott."

"What does he want?" I ask, realizing the time. We've spent the entire day together and I should get home. I have laundry to do and an outline for my civics essay that needs some serious attention.

"It doesn't matter," he says. "No matter what I give Prescott, it's never enough."

"Well, Spencer Beckett, what you gave me last night was plenty."

Spencer laughs. "Is that your way of calling this off?"

I twist my lips. "I just know that there are no guarantees in life. And I don't want to be an obligation."

Spencer draws me to him. We're on the floor, and his arms wrap around mine. "Charlie, I know as well as anyone there are no guarantees. I also know you and I are more than a hook-up."

LATER, when Spencer drops me off at my dorm, I turn to wave goodbye. As I do, snowflakes begin to fall, and my eyes widen.

"You see that?" I ask as Spencer unrolls his window.

"It's beautiful," he says, but his eyes are only on me, his grin not as cocky as before, just filled with...happiness. "Just like you."

I wave at him over my shoulder as I walk away, feeling his gaze on me, butterflies fluttering in my stomach.

We didn't label our relationship, but as I walk to my room a calm sweeps over me. We don't need a label, not now. Because having his word that this is more than a hook-up is enough of a guarantee.

19

SPENCER

"IT'S NON-NEGOTIABLE," Prescott says as he sinks down in a leather club chair to join me. "A bet is a bet."

We're at the Ivy, tumblers of barrel-aged whiskey in hand, and Prescott just won't drop the fucked up bet we made weeks ago.

"I'm not up for it. I've got commitments here that I don't want to break."

"You talking about your waitress? Come on, Charlotte is hot, but so are the hookers in Atlantic City."

"She's not a waitress anymore," I say under my breath. For the last week, I know Charlie has grown more tense over the fact she hasn't found another job. She doesn't want any handouts, which I respect, but it kills me to know she is stressed. I need to figure out a way to help her out without her knowing.

And without my family knowing.

I may be twenty-three, but I'm not financially independent. Not yet. My parents control my trust fund until I finish grad school. And until then, they are aware of all my expenses. If they found out I was financially supporting a woman I've known for less than a month they wouldn't exactly be pleased.

I need to find a way to help Charlie that isn't tied to Beckett money.

"I've known you most of my life, Spence. You have never gone back on your word. You can't start now."

I finish my drink, thinking. "I'm not interested in sex with strangers, but I'd be up for a night at a roulette table."

Prescott claps. "There's my boy. I'll call the limo, you ready to go?"

"Now?" I look at my phone, already knowing the answer It's only seven. It takes less than two hours to get to the strip. "It's a Wednesday night, Prescott."

"Perfect. I'll call the boys." He squeezes my shoulders. "It's time to get lucky, motherfucker."

WHEN WE WALK into the Borgata, I can't help but grin. Prescott is pumped, and Connery and Yates are already drunk. It's been a while since I let loose with my boys, and I admit to feeling their excitement. On the limo ride over they push me for details about Charlotte.

"So you guys together?" Yates pours us another round of bourbon on ice.

"Technically, no, but I can see it going there." I stretch my legs out in front of me, unable to help the smile that tugs at my lips when I think of Charlie.

"That's fucking nuts." Connery shakes his head. "Princeton Charming falling for a commoner."

"You can't be like that," I tell him, holding his gaze and making sure he knows I'm serious. "You have to be cool about her, have my back. God knows my mother is gonna lose her shit."

Yates raises his glass, his words slurred when he says, "To your Princess."

Prescott's jaw twitches and he rolls his eyes, but he raises his glass anyway, playing along. No way is he going to risk ruining tonight by weighing in on anything.

I can't figure out what his deal is with Charlie. He was the one who was trying to get her a job, even though it didn't pan out.

"I tried to pull some strings," Prescott says when I ask him about it.

I've tried not to be jealous that she accepted his help, but not mine. Prescott of all people. I love the man, but he's either hot or cold with her. A nagging feeling in the back of my head thinks he's still pissed that I refused his idea of sharing her.

But no way in hell am I letting her near him. Or near any other man for that matter.

Charlie Hayes is mine.

Prescott shrugs. "Turns out they were unpaid intern positions."

"Unpaid internships reek of privilege. You shouldn't have gotten her hopes up. I mean, who can afford to take that on?"

"Us," he says, smirking.

"We're not getting into a bougie debate on a night where we're playing hundred dollar hands," Yates says, looking between us, obviously feeling the tension.

And I know he's right. There's a time and place for everything.

But by the time we're in the casino, the bottle of

bourbon we finished off in the limo has erased the strain between us. I'm here for one reason and one reason only. To win a fuck ton of cash for Charlie.

We head to the roulette tables, and a cocktail waitress takes our orders as we begin laying down chips. I'm putting my money on odds, because yes, I am cheesy as fuck, and for me and Charlie to work out, it's gonna be against all odds.

The dealer drops the ball on the track and spins the wheel. It lands on twenty-three. "Nice," Prescott says, raising his bourbon. "That's how we do it."

We keep playing for an hour or so, but I see Prescott's eyes constantly scanning the room as if he's looking for something, or someone.

"What gives?" I ask as I place half my chips on black on the outside of the table for a side bet, hoping to double it all. Yates bets on red and I laugh. "You going against me? Man. Brutal!"

Prescott clears his throat. "Ah, nothing, just heard a group from campus might be coming."

I frown. Who else would be here on a Wednesday night. "Who?"

Prescott shrugs. "Doesn't matter, but you need to loosen up. You look so tense every time you make a bet."

I clench my jaw, not interested in sharing my

personal motivation with my oldest friend. Something about him is just not sitting right with me.

Connery walks over to us, arms raised. "The party just arrived, fuckers!"

With him is a clan of five Ivy girls, Winslow at the helm.

"What the hell, Prescott?" I ask, turning toward him as the dealer announces red twelve. *Fuck.*

"Nice," Yates slurs, getting more drunk by the minute, but he just won big.

It's not looking good for me. In fact, this entire night just turned into a clusterfuck.

Winslow is sauntering over to me with a sly look on her face. Long gone is the drunk girl from the post-football victory party, and the pajama-clad Winslow from the grocery store parking lot is nowhere to be seen. Now she is poised to perfection and cold sober. I know because she has that icy look in her eyes she only gets when she hasn't been drinking. Clarity. Decision. Intent.

And she is looking straight at me.

"Let's go dancing," Georgia Renshaw, Winslow's best friend says to Connery, slinging an arm over his shoulder. "Come on, please!?"

Connery has a thing for Georgia and so the

next thing I know, we're all headed to the hotel's dance club.

"It's gonna be dead on a mid-week night," I say, trailing behind the group. I drink my bourbon trying to think how I can ditch my friends for a few hands of blackjack.

"Hey, you're here for a night of debauchery," Prescott says. "If the club is dead, we can bring it to life." He pulls out a plastic baggie of coke from his breast pocket.

"Not my thing, man," I say, unease creeping into my chest. "You know, I'm really not up for dancing. I'll meet up with you later."

Prescott is pissed, but I don't care. The last thing I want is Winslow grinding against me on a dance floor.

I'm just sitting down at a blackjack table when someone reaches around me, covering my eyes.

"Guess who," Winslow laughs as I pull her hands away. She spins my stool around and plops down in my lap. Before I can peel her off of me, she's pulled out her phone and taking photos of us. When a cocktail waitress walks by, Win drags her into the shot. "The more, the merrier," she says playfully.

"Enough," I say, giving the waitress a fifty dollar chip as an apology for Winslow's obnoxious mood.

Winslow slides into the stool next to me. "You're no fun tonight."

"What are you even doing here?"

She frowns as I am dealt in. I look at my cards, not wanting to give her any more attention.

"I came because I was invited. Everyone thought you needed a fun night out with your real friends, to remember what really matters."

I refuse to play along. She's just trying to get under my skin, and I won't let her.

"Listen, Spence, Georgie literally heard that Daphne girl, Charlotte Hayes' roommate, in the dining hall telling people you guys slept together. We are here for damage control."

I scoff, tapping the table for another card. Twenty-one on the money. I take my winnings and leave, not wanting to get into this in front of a dealer. For all her talk, Winslow sure could learn some table manners.

"Damage control? Is that what you call this? Because I call it quits. Seriously, Win, I'm done. You and I, we're over. I told my mom that the other day, and I suggest you let your parents know the same. Go find another rising politician to claim."

Winslow's eyes gloss over, and I can see the tears building.

Shit.

"We're practically family, Spencer. You know that." Her chin trembles, and in her face I see a reel of memories. Our first kiss when we were thirteen. Our first prep school dance. Teaching her to drive on her father's stick shift BMW. Losing our virginity at Nantucket the summer we both turned sixteen.

"You slept with Ethan." I keep my voice cold, void of any emotion.

She swallows hard, and I see the guilt in her eyes, but also the accusal. "What was I supposed to do? You broke my heart, Spencer. After you broke up with me..."

"I never meant to hurt you." And I hadn't. But I knew we would never make each other happy. Still, it didn't mean I still didn't care about her. She was right, we are practically family.

Tears fall down her cheeks and I pull her into my arms. She may not be my last, but she was so many of my firsts.

"I love you, Spencer." She sniffs.

I wipe the tears from her cheek and give her a sad smile. "You love the idea of me, Winnie."

"Can't that be enough?"

I shake my head. "No. Not anymore."

Realizing I'm not backing down, she presses her lips into a firm line and steps away. "You're going to regret this, Spencer."

I let her walk away, knowing she's wrong.

It's time I closed that chapter. I want the fairy tale ending, and it won't be with Winslow Harrington.

20

CHARLIE

"So you guys are over?" Daphne asks as we stand in line for caffeine at a campus coffee stand. We have the same eight am class on Thursdays, and it just finished. We didn't have time to get coffee before class started, but now we are desperate. I'm going to need an extra large dark roast to get through the day.

I was up half the night studying for the Theories of Global Justice test I have today.

"Hmm?" I ask, not really paying attention to my roommate.

With her phone in hand she repeats, "You and Spencer Beckett, you guys aren't like a thing anymore?"

Leaning in so the people behind us don't hear I

whisper, "We haven't labeled the relationship, but we're a thing. I mean, I think we're a thing."

She twists her lips. "Um, you should have a look at this then."

Before I can glance at her phone, the barista asks to take our order. But I don't get a chance to order my basic black drip coffee before Daphne asks for two extra large, extra shot, peppermint mochas as she hands over her credit card.

"'Tis the season," she says as we walk to the queue to wait for our drinks.

"Thank you," I say, shoving my crumpled one dollar bills back in my purse. I rewrap the scarf around my neck and wiggle my toes. The temperature seems to have dropped ten degrees overnight. Christmas is inching closer and closer and I am no nearer to sorting out how I'm going to get home. "Now what were you saying?"

"Don't get upset, but..." She hands me her phone.

I frown as I look at some guy named Yates Bradford. The image is of him at a dance club with a bunch of semi-familiar looking girls. "Who is this?"

"Oops, this one," she says, swiping up.

My stomach drops.

"Wait, when was this taken?" I ask, zooming in on the image of Spencer Beckett and Winslow Harrington. The photo is tagged in Atlantic City. Winslow's arms are wrapped around him, and he's cupping her face with his hand. They are mere inches apart with a blackjack table behind them, and they look...intimate.

Daphne places her hand on my arm and gives it a small squeeze. "It was posted late last night."

My heart sinks. "Are you sure? How did you even find this?"

"Two peppermint mochas," the barista calls out and Daphne grabs our drinks just as Tatum approaches us.

"Hey ladies," he says, draping his arms around our shoulders. "It's fucking cold as balls out there."

I bite my lip, scared I'm going to start crying. Daphne notices and takes control. "Um, we're in crisis mode." She grabs her phone and shows Tatum.

"Oh, shit, Hayes."

Daphne nods. "Exactly. We need carbs. Pancake carbs. Now."

"Your next class isn't for an hour and a half, right?" he asks, looking at me, but he already knows the answer.

Numb, a million emotions and thoughts clamoring inside me, I let them lead me out of the coffee shop.

Don't cry, Charlie, I warn myself. *You knew what you were getting into when you hooked up with Spencer Beckett.*

But I'd still let myself fall for Princeton Charming, even knowing how it would end.

Ten minutes later we slide into a booth at an off-campus diner and I focus on drinking my mocha as Tatum and Daphne order for the table.

"Are there any more photos?" I ask when the waitress leaves. My voice sounds distant, metallic, detached.

Tatum and Daphne share a look.

"What? If there are, just show me so we can get this over with."

Daphne hands me her phone again, this time it's Winslow's Instagram feed. There are half a dozen photos of her in Spencer's lap. Her arms are around him, and in some of them, another woman is with them too. She's captioned it, *Double the fun.*

My stomach turns.

"I really thought. I mean, he seemed so sincere." *Don't cry, don't cry.* But I can feel the stupid tears forming, burning my eyes.

"The guy's a player. What did you expect?" Tatum says.

"Not helpful." Daphne smacks his shoulder.

"What? I tried to warn her—"

"I can't do this right now." I push out of my seat. "I have to go."

Both Tatum and Daphne call after me, but I dart out of the restaurant, and when I'm finally outside and I know they aren't following me, I let my tears fall.

"He's just a guy," I mumble. "Just a stupid, asshole, inconsiderate—"

"Charlie?" Ava, Spencer's younger sister, is waving at me from the steps of one of the campus buildings. "Hey, wait up."

Not now. I haven't seen her since the night at the hospital. As she approaches, her smile drops.

"Are you all right?"

"Yeah, I'm just in a rush to get to class." A small lie.

She doesn't look like she believes me. "I hope it's not something my idiot brother did."

I laugh at that, but there's no humor in it. I just need my space. Time to process that the guy I gave my heart and body to isn't who I thought he was.

Spencer Beckett is the ultimate player...and he did a good job playing me.

"I never got the chance to say thank you for helping me that night." She winces. "It's pretty embarrassing."

"I'm just glad you were okay. But I should really go."

"Sure. But maybe we can have coffee sometime? Now that you and Spencer are dating—"

"We're not." The words come out clipped because I'm trying to hold back my tears again.

"Oh, I thought..." Her brows are drawn down. "He cares about you. I don't think I've ever seen him so into someone. He even..." She chews on her bottom lip before saying. "It's probably for the best. You're sweet, Charlotte." She winces. "And in our world, sweet gets eaten alive. I love my brother, but he'll hurt you even if he doesn't want to."

I know she's not trying to be mean. I can see the concern in her eyes. But I'm reminded once again that I'm not good enough for Spencer Beckett.

"Hayes," a deep voice says behind me, filled with something that sounds like triumph. Prescott slings a heavy arm over my shoulder then says to Ava. "And little Beckett. What are the two of you scheming about?"

I shrug him off. "I was just leaving." I say to Ava before I walk away, "Thanks for the advice."

Anger has replaced all sadness as I start to jog toward the building where my class is. So when Prescott catches up to me and spins me around, I can barely control my response.

"What do you want, Prescott? To rub my face in those pictures?"

He fucking grins at me. "So you saw them already. News travels fast. I tried to warn you—"

"Right. I need to watch my back, right?" I repeat the words he said to me at the coffee shop a couple weeks ago. "What was the other thing, about a bet? Were you both playing me the entire time?"

He leans closer. "I enjoy games, Charlotte. They make life interesting. Blackjack, roulette...And you." There's something dark in his gaze as it focuses on me. "You were a bet I knew I'd win."

"You didn't win anything."

He chuckles. "I knew you'd never go home with Beckett that night at the gala. So yeah, Hayes, I won. A night in Atlantic City, all paid thanks to Spencer Beckett's inability to walk away from a challenge."

That's what I was to him - a bet, a challenge.

"You're an asshole, you know that," I spit out, turning to walk away.

He steps in front of me. "It should be Beckett you're pissed at, doll. I'm not the one who fucked you over." He winks, expression filled with lascivious suggestions. "Even though I wanted to. If you want to get back at Beckett, I can think of a way that will benefit us both."

I have to squeeze my fists to my side in order not to slap him. "Get out of my way, Prescott."

"What? You think you're too good for me?" He sneers, grabbing my arms. "I've got deeper pockets and a bigger cock than—"

I don't see Spencer approach, and I'm pretty sure Prescott doesn't either, because one second he's leering over me, and the next he sprawled out on the lawn in front of me. Spencer has him by the collar of his jacket, his fist inches from Prescott's face. I can't hear what he says, but from the tone I know it's a threat.

"You're brainwashed because of a little virgin pussy," Prescott says, loud enough for me and the small crowd that's started to gather around to watch. He pushes Spencer away and they both stand.

"Just stay away from her or we're done."

"You're losing it, Beckett. I get the need to slum it every once in awhile, but——"

Spencer raises his arm, and I know he's about to punch his best friend in the face. And while I'd really like to see it, I know it won't solve anything.

"Spencer, stop."

Mid-swing, he stops, his breathing heavy, eyes wild as they pin Prescott with a murderous look.

"Just stop," I repeat, my own breathing coming out labored. Confusion, frustration, anger, the swirl like an out of control vortex inside me. I haven't even begun to process the pictures of Spencer and Winslow together, let alone Prescott's words, or Spencer swooping in like a dark knight willing to protect my honor.

But it's him I need protection from.

The crowd has grown bigger now, and I notice more than a few phones are out.

Without another word, I turn and run. I know I'm forgetting something. But I can't remember what. And right now I don't care. I just need to find a dark cave to burrow myself in and cry. Tears blur my vision, and I have no idea where I'm going. I just need to get away.

21

SPENCER

"You're really going to throw away a lifetime of friendship for some cheap pussy?" Prescott growls out, lip curled over his teeth.

I'm ready to take another swing at him when I realize Charlie has taken off.

"Friends don't fuck each other over." I turn to chase after her, ignoring Prescott's comments that trail after me.

"You'll thank me when this is all over."

Bullshit. He's lucky Charlie stopped me mid swing from bashing his front teeth out of his head. I still have an itch to turn around and do it.

I knew the second I woke up this morning and saw the photos posted on Winslow's Instagram that trouble was brewing. I'd gone straight to Charlie's dorm to explain before she saw them, but she was already gone.

Half the morning I'd driven around campus trying to find her. It was Ava who finally helped me figure out where she was.

Brat: What did you do to Charlie? You're a real douche, you know that?

Me: You saw her?

Brat: I was just talking to her. She seemed really upset.

Me: Text me your exact location.

She had. But it wasn't Ava I'd found her with. Prescott was hovering over her, his posture meant to intimidate, but it was his words that sent me over the edge.

And now she's gone again, and I can't imagine what she's thinking.

I text Winslow as I walk toward where I parked my car.

Me: You went too far this time. We're done for good. And stay the hell away from Charlie, or I'll ruin you.

Fear rather than anger guide me. Because I know I may have just lost Charlie forever.

And I wouldn't blame her if she never wants anything to do with me again, because this shit, the pictures, Prescott's interfering, the way my friends and family think they can use other people as pawns to get what they want - it's my fucked up life.

It's starting to snow, and as I turn onto Prospect Ave., I see her. Shoulders hunched over, scarf wrapped around her face, I know it's Charlie. I start to slow and roll the window down.

"Charlie."

She glances over and I see her eyes are bloodshot and puffy from crying. "Go away, Spencer, I have nothing to say to you."

"Let me explain. Get in the car."

"I don't care what you have to say. Prescott explained everything."

"I don't know what Prescott's fucking problem is, but I'll deal with him. He had no right talking to you like that."

She stops walking and turns on me. "You think you're any different? You and he are the same. You think just because you have money you can use people any way you want."

"You're right. I was that way, but not anymore. Not with you."

She bites her bottom lip and I can see she's holding back tears. "I can't do this. Just leave me alone."

When she starts to walk away, I get out of the car, slamming the door before moving around the hood and pulling her toward me.

"Let me go, Spencer."

"Not until you listen to me. I know what those pictures looked like, but nothing happened. She was all over me, snapping pictures before I had a chance to push her away. I had no clue she was even going to be there. Pretty sure Prescott set the whole thing up."

"Even if that's true, don't you see how messed up that is?"

"I know. Just come back to my place. Please, Charlie." I have her face in my hands, pleading with her with my words and eyes. "I don't want to lose you."

Her bottom lip trembles and I'm terrified she's going to say no, that she'll walk away for good. But after a few shaky breaths, she nods.

"I'm going to make this up to you," I say, opening the passenger side door and helping her in.

She's silent as we drive back to my place, and when I take her hand she doesn't pull away, but she doesn't relax into my touch like she usually does. There's tension in her, and her silence scares me more than her angry words.

I know I should just let her go. As much as I want to protect her from people like Prescott and Winslow, I know if she's going to be part of my life, there will always be people trying to get between us.

Even my own mother would rather see me miserable than be with someone like Charlie.

"It's fucked up," I mutter, tossing my keys on the table as we enter my apartment.

Charlie still hasn't said anything, but she looks at me as I take her jacket, and there's so much uncertainty and doubt in her eyes it makes my chest squeeze painfully.

"*I* fucked up," I say, pressing my forehead to hers. "I should have known Winslow would pull something like that. But you have to believe me that nothing happened between us. You're who I want, Charlie."

She gives a small shake of her head. "I don't know if I can do this. I care about you Spencer—"

"That's all that matters." I kiss her, hard, possessive, probably demanding more than she can give right now, but I need to know that she's still mine.

That I haven't lost her.

"Spencer," she whimpers against my lips, her body melting into mine.

Maybe it makes me even more of an asshole,

knowing the power my touch has over her and using it to prevent her from walking away. But I need her.

I lift her up, wrapping her legs around my waist and carrying her to my bedroom.

"This doesn't solve anything," she says against my mouth, even though her hands are already tugging at my shirt, and her body vibrates with anticipation.

I lay her down on my bed, kissing her as I peel off her clothes. "You're mine, Charlie Hayes." She whimpers as I kiss her breast. "That's what it solves."

"You're going to break my heart."

"I won't."

She closes her eyes then, and I know she is struggling to believe me, to trust me.

"Let me try to be the man you need," I ask as I run my bare hands over her skin. Her nipples are hard, and I swirl my tongue around them, my cock growing with need as I melt against her body.

"Oh Spence," she moans, running her fingers through my hair. Her legs open for me and I slip my fingers inside her, needing to feel her tight warmth. "Make me come." Her words tell me that even if she's upset, she can separate all that from what we share.

My fingers move against her, her slick entrance getting my cock nice and ready. As her hand wraps around my shaft I kiss her hard, I kiss her knowing that this is exactly what I want. And in this moment, I know it's what she wants too.

It seems everything in my life is trying to sabotage us, but there is nothing that can get between us right now. In my room, the world grows small. Her and me. Nothing else. Just this.

"Charlie," I whisper her name as I fill her up, my hands on her ass, her hips, easing her against me until she is moaning my name.

"Oh God, Spence," she whimpers as I move deeper inside her. Her warm pussy is so wet and ready that when I fill her up entirely, she begins to cry out for relief. "Make me come, oh God, yes, yes, ohhh." She wraps her legs tight around me as she comes, and I find myself holding onto her as I finish. I drop my mouth to hers, needing her sweet lips, needing her warm body. Needing her.

Her.

Only her.

"God, I like kissing you."

She smiles, the dark hurt in her eyes from earlier

is fading, and she looks up at me with a depth we haven't shared before. "Coming from you, that is quite the compliment," she says. Then she rolls me over, onto my back. "But I need more than kisses, Spencer Beckett. I need you to fuck me until I forget about those photos."

Her hair falls in her face and I tuck the strands behind her ears. "Is that the healthiest way to deal with pain?" I ask.

She twists her lips. "Haha," she says sarcastically. "I just want to feel good right now. That's all. No psychoanalysis necessary."

She runs her hands over my tight balls, and I groan. "I guess sex isn't the worst way to get over our first fight."

She smirks as she lifts her ass, sinking against my already hard cock. "You think that was our first fight?" she laughs.

I chuckle, my hands on her hips. "Oh right, you started this off by throwing champagne in my face."

She swivels her hips, her perfect tits bouncing as she does, making me feel like the luckiest man at Princeton. "I'd do it all again," she murmurs. "*That* was totally worth *this*."

I KISS her once more before rolling out of bed. "I have a class this afternoon. After I shower, we can have a quick lunch, then I'll drop you back off at campus."

"Oh God." She sits up and throws back the sheets, her eyes wide with panic as she searches frantically for her clothes. "No, no, no. This can't be happening."

"What's wrong?"

"I have a test." She reaches for her phone and lets out a small whimper when she looks at the time. "I missed it."

"It's okay, I'm sure you'll be able to get the prof to give you a make-up."

She shoves her legs into her jeans and haphazardly throws on her shirt. "I can't believe I forgot. I've never..." She's half under my bed looking for something.

I find her second shoe. "Is this what you're looking for?"

Standing, she takes it from my hand and starts to dart out of the bedroom.

"I have to go. If I can catch Professor Jenkins before she leaves, maybe she'll let me—"

"Charlie, wait. Let me get dressed and I'll drive you."

"No. I'll just..." There are those damn tears again.

"I get that you're upset, but it's just one test."

"It's not just a test, Spencer. It's my life. A life that you've railroaded since the moment I saw you."

"Charlie—"

"No. I have to go."

"Call me after?" I ask, not caring that there is a hint of desperation in my voice. "We can get dinner and drinks, do something cool—"

She cuts me off. "See, that's the problem, Spence. It's all cocktails and fun for you. But that isn't the real world. And that's why when you take out the attraction we have for one another there isn't anything left."

"You're wrong, Charlie," I say, my chest tight. "We're so much more than sex."

"Maybe, but right now Spencer, I can't afford to find out if you're right."

22

CHARLIE

I SPEND my last twenty on a taxi back to campus, but when I get to the lecture hall, Professor Jenkins is gone. She's also not in her office. So not knowing what else to do, I head back to my dorm.

Thankfully, Daphne isn't there.

But another note is tucked under the door when I walk in, my name scribbled across the front.

My throat constricts when I read the words inside.

Glass slippers aren't the only thing that break, Cinderella. Next time remember your place or your fall will be a lot worse.

Anger overrides any fear I should probably feel and I crumple the paper into a ball and toss it in the wastebasket beside my desk. But after a day like today, this stalker-thing isn't even on my radar.

Whoever it is obviously doesn't want me anywhere near Spencer. Which narrows it down to about...well, the entire campus.

I flop onto my bed and pull the comforter over my shoulders. It's not the time to fall apart. I should be writing an email to the professor and finishing my essay that's due next week - anything but thinking about Princeton Charming.

But that's exactly where my head goes.

We're so much more than sex. Spencer's words echo in my head.

I actually believe he thinks he's giving me his all - and maybe he is. Maybe he does feel more for me than just the chemistry between us. But I don't know if it's enough.

Honestly, I'm starting to think that I'm not strong enough to deal with the assholes in his life. The drama. The feeling like I don't measure up. But then Spencer looks at me, touches me, and I come completely undone. It's unnatural, the power he has over my heart and body.

I've never felt this confused before. My head feels like I've been on one of those roundabouts I used to play on at the park when I was a kid. When you're on it, spinning, spinning, spinning, your heart races, and there's excitement and a little bit of fear. But when you get off, the world gets all jumbled, and you feel like you're going to be sick - that's what happens when I'm away from Spencer. And I know I have two options, to get back on the roundabout, or to walk away and wait for the world to finally make sense again.

Walk away, Charlie, my head demands.

Get back on, my heart and body plead.

I groan, digging my palms into my eyes. I wish I was home, with one of Dad's steaming cups of cocoa and Mom to snuggle against and tell her all my worries. I want to tell her everything, but if I call I'm going to have to finally stop putting off the inevitable and tell them that I can't come home for Christmas.

"Hey, there you are," Daphne says as she walks into the room. "I was getting worried about you. Tatum said you never showed for your test. And then I heard about the scene with Prescott and Spencer. Are you all right?"

Sitting up, I lean against my headboard, I wrap my arms around my chest. "No. Not even a little."

She sits down on the edge of my bed. "Want to talk about it?"

"I'm just so confused."

"What you need is a girl's night out. My treat."

"That's the last thing I need right now."

"You can't let a boy bring you down like this. Best medicine for a broken heart is to get pissed drunk with your best friend." She grins at me. "And get right back on the saddle. I've got the perfect guy for you—"

"Spencer and I aren't really broken up."

"You're kidding, right?" She looks absolutely mortified. "But he cheated on you. Where's your pride?"

"He didn't—"

My phone starts to ring, and I dig through my backpack until I find it. I frown when I see my dad's cell number, but talking to him is less daunting than facing the angry stare down from Daphne.

"Hey, Dad."

"Hey, peanut." His voice is strained, and he sounds like he hasn't slept in awhile.

"Is everything all right?"

Silence.

"Dad?" Nerves scatter across my flesh causing goosebumps to rise on my arms. "What's wrong?"

"I didn't want you to worry, sweetheart, but

215

your mom isn't doing well. She's back in the hospital. She has pneumonia—"

"Oh no."

"Baby girl, I think you need to come home."

Grief. Fear. They strangle me, because I know the only way he'd ever ask me to come home is if…I can't think about it.

"Okay. I'll…" I don't have enough for a plane ticket, and even a one-way bus ticket will be hard to pay for. But I have to find a way. "I'll be home as soon as I can. I love you, Daddy."

"Love you too, Charlie bear," he chokes on the words before he ends the call.

"I have to go home…" I push myself off my bed and grab my suitcase from under my bed, then start shoving my clothes into it.

"What happened?" Daphne is beside me.

"My mom—" I bite my bottom lip hard, trying to stop the tears that burn my eyes. I can't lose her.

"Is it her MS again?"

I manage to nod, not even looking at what I'm doing. Everything I own can fit in that one bag, and in a way I'm grateful. Because I don't know when or if I'll be back.

"Oh, sweetheart." She hugs me and I let her,

even though I want to keep moving. I'll walk home if I have to. "I'm sorry."

"I...just need..." I cover my face with my hands. "I don't know how I'm going to pay for a damn ticket. I lost my job, and I just used my last twenty to pay for a taxi..." God, I wish I could go back to the night I tossed champagne in Spencer's face and change things.

"How much do you need?"

"I'm not taking your money, Daph. I don't know when I'll be able to pay you back."

She shrugs and moves to her bed, pulling out a fistful of bills from her wallet. "I still haven't bought your Christmas gift yet. So consider this your present." She places the bills in my hand.

"It's too much." And yet it's just enough to get me on a red-eye to Detroit.

"I may not be Spencer Beckett rich, but I can afford to help you out."

I know I shouldn't take it. There are always strings attached with Daphne. But honestly, I don't know what else to do.

"Thank you. I promise I'll pay you back."

"I know you will," she says, her smile a little too big.

But my suspicion radar is off the charts after today.

All I know for certain is I have to get home.

I start to text Spencer but stop myself. I can't deal with him right now, and I know if I call him, he'll be here in a heartbeat, throwing his money around and trying to fix things. And as much as I want his arms around me, his strength, his words that everything will be alright, I know that it won't be.

In my world, people get sick, jobs are lost, and moms die.

I'm not Cinderella.

And Spencer isn't my prince.

Kissing Princeton Charming was fun while it lasted.

But it's finally time I wake up and remember that this isn't a damn fairy tale.

23

SPENCER

"CHARLIE, CALL ME BACK," I say to her voice message for the third time since she left my place yesterday afternoon. "I'm getting worried."

I waited outside her Poli-Sci class, but she never came out. She's usually with Tatum afterward, but he's got a redhead hanging off his arms as he walks out of the building.

He frowns when he sees me. "What do you want?"

"I'm trying to find Charlie. Have you talked to her?"

"Wouldn't tell you if I had. You hurt her. Lucky I don't give you a beat down."

The redhead gasps, looking between us. But

even as she feigns shock, I see her gaze run down my body appreciatively.

I hold back the eye roll that I want to unleash on both of them.

"Charlie and I are good."

"If that was the case you wouldn't be here asking me where she is."

He has a point. But even though I knew she was upset when she left my place, I thought we had made strides to make things work.

I walk toward Charlie's dorm, calling her again, and cursing when it goes straight to voicemail.

"I don't know why you're ignoring me..." I pinch the bridge of my nose. "Okay, I get why you are. But don't ignore me, Charlie. We can work through this. I..."

I need her. It's pathetic, but it's the truth. And yet as I walk down the hall of her dorm toward her room, there's a pressure on the back of my skull. Maybe it's a premonition, a knowing. Whatever it is, I hesitate before knocking.

When the door opens, I have a second of hope, before I see it's Daphne and not Charlie on the other side.

"What do you want?"

I'm getting a little sick of people asking me that. Treating me like I'm the fucking devil himself.

"I need to speak to Charlie."

"She's not here." The blonde crosses her arms and glares daggers at me.

"Do you know when she'll be back?"

"No."

More silence, more daggers.

"Look, I know you're trying to protect her, but I'm worried. She wasn't in class today, and Charlie doesn't skip—"

"She's gone, Spencer."

"Gone?" My heart sinks. "Gone where?"

She hesitates before sighing and answering, "Home."

"Why?"

"Does it matter? You need to leave her alone. She's gone. If she wanted to talk to you, she would have called. That she didn't, proves she doesn't want anything to do with you."

"Please, Daphne, call her and tell her I need to talk."

Daphne purses her lips. "No way, I'm not letting you stress her out at a time like this."

I'm so pissed I could punch a wall. Turning, I

head for the stairwell. There is no getting through to Daphne.

As I walk toward the landing, I am so consumed with Charlie that I bump into someone. "Shit, I'm sorry," I say as I knock a bucket of cleaning supplies from the woman's hand and onto the floor.

"Oh it's fine," she says, reaching for the bucket the same time I do. We knock heads.

"Fuck, sorry." I hand it to her, feeling like I'm on the verge of fucking tears.

"Hey, are you Spencer Beckett?" she asks.

I nod, running a hand over my neck. "Yeah, sorry again." I start to walk away, but she calls me back.

"You were dating Charlotte, right?"

Were.

No. *Are.* At least if I have a say in it.

"Yeah." I turn to her. "You're friends?"

"Yeah, I'm Jill," she says, sticking out her hand.

I register the name and remember Charlie telling me it was Jill she traded work shifts with sometimes.

"Have you heard from her today?" I ask.

I almost tell her that she won't call me back, but I bite my tongue, hoping she'll unknowingly give me information. Unethical maybe, but what would anyone expect from Spencer Fucking Beckett? I work people, isn't that how I got this bullshit nickname in the first place?

Jill gives my arm a sympathetic squeeze. "It's awful, isn't it? To have her mom back in the hospital at Christmas? And today she texted saying she wasn't coming back next semester. It makes me hate the one percent." She grimaces after that last line, then gives me an awkward smile. "No offense."

I raise my hands. "None taken."

Jill exhales. "But a girl like Charlie shouldn't have to drop out to help pay her mom's medical expenses."

"No," I say. "She shouldn't." My mind is swirling with ideas. I've got to get Charlie back here. She shouldn't carry all this on her own.

But she would say that is exactly what privileged Ivy League royalty would say.

Jill gives me a half-smile. "Well, try and have a good Christmas. Once the campus clears out tomorrow, I'll be on cleaning duty." She lifts her buckets and gives me a small wave goodbye.

Jill is going to be cleaning the dorms all winter break. Charlie is going to be keeping vigil at the hospital. And me? My family celebrates Christmas with a decadent brunch with their closest fifty friends and then rings in the New Year in a Manhattan penthouse.

Except maybe not this year.

This year I am finding Charlie Hayes.

Kissing her wasn't enough. I need to date her, to prove to her I am more than Princeton Charming.

I am her happily-ever-after.

She just doesn't know it yet.

C.M. SEABROOK

Amazon bestselling author C.M. Seabrook writes hot, steamy romances with possessive bad boys, and the passionate, fiery women who love them. Swoon-worthy romances from the heart!

For something a little different, read Chantel Seabrook's Shifter, Reverse Harem, and Fantasy books here https://amzn.to/2MTiItI

SIGN UP FOR C.M. Seabrook's NEWSLETTER FOR LATEST NEWS!

Copy and paste the following link: http://eepurl.com/cB56an

Join her FB group for giveaways and more! www.facebook.com/groups/cmseabrook/

She loves to hear from her readers and can be reached at cm.seabrook.books@gmail.com

Melting Steel

FRANKIE LOVE

Frankie Love writes sexy stories about bad boys and mountain men. As a thirty-something mom who is ridiculously in love with her own bearded hottie, she believes in love-at-first-sight and happily-ever-afters. She also believes in the power of a quickie.

Find Frankie here:
www.frankielove.net
frankieloveromance@gmail.com

JOIN FRANKIE LOVE'S
MAILING LIST

AND NEVER MISS A RELEASE!

The Mountain Man's Babies

TIMBER

BUCKED

WILDER

HONORED

CHERISHED

BUILT

CHISELED

HOMEWARD

SIX MEN OF ALASKA

The Wife Lottery

The Wife Protectors

The Wife Gamble

The Wife Code

The Wife Pact

The Wife Legacy

MOUNTAIN MEN OF LINESWORTH

MOUNTAIN MAN CANDY

MOUNTAIN MAN CAKE

MOUNTAIN MAN BUN

#OBSESSED

MOUNTAIN MEN OF BEAR VALLEY

Untamed Virgins

Untamed Lovers

Untamed Daddy

Untamed Fiance

Stand-Alone Romance

B.I.L.F.

BEAUTY AND THE MOUNTAIN MAN

HIS Everything

HIS BILLION DOLLAR SECRET BABY

UNTAMED

RUGGED

HIS MAKE BELIEVE BRIDE

HIS KINKY VIRGIN

WILD AND TRUE

BIG BAD WOLF

MISTLETOE MOUNTAIN: A MOUNTAIN MAN'S CHRISTMAS

Our Virgin

Protecting Our Virgin

Craving Our Virgin

Forever Our Virgin

F*ck Club

A-List F*ck Club

Small Town F*ck Club

Modern-Mail Order Brides

CLAIMED BY THE MOUNTAIN MAN

ORDERED BY THE MOUNTAIN MAN

WIFED BY THE MOUNTAIN MAN

EXPLORED BY THE MOUNTAIN MAN

CROWN ME

COURTED BY THE MOUNTAIN PRINCE

CHARMED BY THE MOUNTAIN PRINCE

CROWNED BY THE MOUNTAIN PRINCE

CROWN ME, PRINCE: The Complete Collection

Las Vegas Bad Boys

ACE

KING

MCQUEEN

JACK

Los Angeles Bad Boys

COLD HARD CASH

HOLLYWOOD HOLDEN

SAINT JUDE

THE COMPLETE COLLECTION

Made in the USA
San Bernardino, CA
15 January 2019